Powerful praise for
KIRK ALEX
& his various novels, short stories & anthologies

Ziggy Popper at Large
(crime noir single)

"★★★★1/2 out of five."

—goodreads.com

"★★★★ out of five."

—Barnes & Noble

Working the Hard Side of the Street —
Selected Stories / Poems / Screams

". . . this is a nicely put together piece of work."

—BookLore

"City of Angels? Maybe for that couple of percent of people who get anywhere near that thing called 'fame and fortune.' Everyone else is just trying to get by in a place where, if you don't have the right job and a flashy car, the odds are very much stacked against you.

"This book is excellent. It's full of honest, heartfelt writing that certainly shows a very different view of Hollywood."

—Paul Lappen, *DEAD TREES REVIEW*

**WORKING THE HARD SIDE OF THE STREET —
L.A. Cab Stories, Vol. I**

"★★★★1/2 out of five."

—amazon

"WORKING THE HARD SIDE OF THE STREET— Selected Stories / Poems / Screams is an anthology of powerful, caustic, original tales and poems by Kirk Alex about the ups, downs, and hard knocks of Hollywood's seamy underbelly. The perspective of a "fly- on-the-wall" cab driver provides a piercing realism and insight into the vicious clashes and personal struggles that lie hidden underneath the entertainment capital's glossy, photo-touched exterior. WORKING THE HARD SIDE OF THE STREET is recommended as a gut-wrenching read for both its candor and bravado."

—THE MIDWEST BOOK REVIEW

**BLOOD, SWEAT and CHUMP CHANGE —
Taxi Tales & Vignettes**

"After reading BLOOD, SWEAT AND CHUMP CHANGE— Taxi Tales & Vignettes by Kirk Alex you understand why the American Dream needs lipo suction. It's all here: Hate, poetry, sadness, hope and the ache of an aloneness that never goes away. Belly up!"

—Dan Fante, author of *Mooch* and *Spitting Off Tall Buildings*

**nonentity
A Novel**

"Jack Kerouac knew some little bit about the road. So does Kirk Alex. You can digest this book in two hours — it will stay with you forever."
—Steve Rosen, *Curled Up With A Good Book*

"This is another well done, honest and heartfelt piece of writing from Kirk Alex. At one time or another, everyone can identify with Chance, being unemployed and very low on funds. It's short, easy to read, and well worth the reader's time."
—Paul Lappen, *DEAD TREES REVIEW*

**Fifty Shades of Tinsel
(Portrait of a Heartthrob)
A Novel**

"This story is a bit dark and to say there is a lot of sex is an understatement. Jimmy's journey is an interesting one. ★★★★ out of five."
—NetGalley

LUSTMORD: Anatomy of a Serial Butcher
Boxed Set/Complete Series

"★★★★ out of five."

—amazon

Bone: A Choo-Choo Buschitski Crime Noire Single

"★★★★ out of five."

—amazon

BY KIRK ALEX

Lustmord: Anatomy of a Serial Butcher

Zook

Throwback — **Book One (of Two)** — **Love, Lust & Murder Series**

Backlash — Book Two (of Two) — Love, Lust & Murder Series

Fifty Shades of Tinsel

nonentity

Working the Hard Side of the Street —
Selected Stories/Poems/Screams

Blood, Sweat & Chump Change — Taxi Tales & Vignettes

Ziggy Popper at Large — Story Collection

Hush-Hush — Holiday #1

Hubba-Hubba — Holiday #2

Hard Noir — Holiday #3

ZIGGY POPPER

AT LARGE

14 TALES OF GENERAL DEGENERACY, OF MAYHEM & DEBAUCHERY — FOR THE MORALLY CONFLICTED & BORDERLINE CRIMINAL

KIRK ALEX

TUCUMCARI PRESS

Tucson – 2017

Ziggy Popper at Large — 14 Tales of General Degeneracy, of Mayhem & Debauchery — for the Morally Conflicted & Borderline Criminal is a work of fiction. Names, characters, places and incidents are either the product of the author's imagination or are used fictitiously. Any resemblance to actual persons, living or dead, or to actual events or locales is entirely coincidental.

ISBN: 978-0-939122-75-2 (6x9 paperback)
ISBN: 978-0-939122-76-9 (eBook)

Contents

Ziggy Popper at Large

The joint wasn't much. They had an old juke, planks for shelves and not much booze in evidence on those shelves, either. Dive was being remodeled or something. So they claimed. Yeah. Sure. But it was a hot mother of an afternoon out there and East Hollywood was getting its ass whipped. There were three or four other losers in the bar beside myself, sucking down suds, wiping sweat, belching and farting. The air-conditioning was on the fritz and they had the front door open, and I kept either looking down at my beer or staring out the door so as not to have to look at the greasy barkeep while he picked his nose or played with the fucking fly swatter. But I was safe; I had asked to open the bottle myself. I kept looking out there, watching the heat and the dust dancing in the smog.

The noisy station wagon he pulled up in was pretty banged up and so was he. About 5'11", big nose, scrawny and ugly. But the son of a bitch had a shit-eating grin on his face and that didn't make any sense to me at all. I turned away and pulled on my bottle. The guy sat on the rickety stool next to mine, ordered a beer and offered to buy me one as well.

What was up? Did this fruit fly just buy me a beer?

"Thanks," I said.

The beer arrived, and the guy said: "You're not married, are you?"

I shook my head. "No fucking way."

He let on how he didn't blame me, because he had a wife who was nothing but a pain in the ass. He'd been married too many years to think about, didn't do much, wrote poetry that nobody wanted. The wife supported them, worked as a nurse, but she really didn't have to work, on account her daddy had money.

It was bullshit. I knew it. But the beer was free. I kept nodding, pulled on the bottle. Sweat poured. It was hot. The ice cold brew hit the spot just right.

"I've done some pornos," he said. "You know, appeared in one or two."

I didn't say anything.

"It's not all it's cracked up to be," he said. "It's a lot of pussy, but most of it is gutter gash. Broads got all the power in the business; men are treated like shit. It don't matter how much you got and can get wood on cue, you're still a second-class citizen. Pussy rules. With pussy comes power. And they wonder why a guy can't get it up."

Some more nonsense that didn't add up. Some were getting so much ass they didn't know what to do with it, and you had others dreaming and hoping and pumping their calloused hand every night. But that's the way it went. The woman I was staying with wasn't into fucking all that much. She was a third-rate stripper on her way down, overweight and burned out—at thirty-eight, with some emotional instability thrown in. But all she needed was a friend and I was a friend and for that she'd give me second-rate head now and then, discussions that went nowhere and screams and cries in the wee hours of the night because she knew she had blown it somewhere along the way and didn't quite know where and now the end of the road was clearly in sight and she had nothing to smile about. I put up with it because I had nowhere else to go. I was doing odd jobs, collecting food stamps. Had succumbed to the flow, and was willingly going along with it. I toyed with the idea of leaving LA, of escaping the sewer, that's what it was, and her screams, but like so many other plans and ideas, I knew it would never happen. No guts. No more. Not lately, anyway. No get-up and go. I guess deep down I knew there was no place *to go*, nowhere; the crap followed you no matter where you went.

The scrawny one went on about porn and the kinds of pigs he'd fucked, not strictly for money, he said, for the poetry, for the experience. It was then I belched. I had a genuine asshole sitting next to me.

He ordered another round and, in an offhand way, asked if I'd fuck his wife if he paid me to do it. I looked at the guy, not too long—turds like this I was used to. So he couldn't get it up, tired of banging the same pussy, and admitted to both.

"What's she look like?" I asked.

The photo in his wallet was old and worn, dog-eared. Woman was lying face down on a brass bed, nothing on but a blindfold. She had turned her head back to look at the camera, but that blindfold and ball-gag in her craw made it difficult to make out much.

"I don't know, man," I said.

"She's not bad looking," he said. "Take my word for it. Got a nice body, good legs. A blind man could see it. Takes care of herself."

"How old?" I said.

"Thirty-six."

I was thinking. And when he produced two twenties, that helped my thinking along. I stuffed the dough in my pocket.

"Half now, half at the other end," he said.

"I get the clap or anything like that, I'll be back and I'll break both your fucking arms."

"She's clean, my friend. I swear. Takes care of herself. She's a nurse, for Chrissake's."

"A nurse, huh?"

"Well, a dental assistant. Same thing."

"Two more twenties later?"

"Got my word. *Good as gold.*"

He gave me the address, in the Miracle Mile. Said the door would be unlocked, then added that she was tied to the bed, spread-eagle, and had been blindfolded—just like in the Polaroid.

"You got it, baby," I told him. "As long as she stays face down so I don't have to see her mug."

"She's not bad looking; I'm telling you, man."

"Fuck it; what difference does it make?"

He shrugged. "Right," he said. Pulled on his bottle, and wasn't looking at me when he added: "I hope you got more than four inches."

"How about twice that, and then some? That okay?"

"No shit; you got that much?"

No, I didn't, only it wasn't any of the punk's business. He was nodding his head, saying: "I had you pegged right. You got the equipment. Yeah, yeah—fine. She'll like that. Is it nice and thick, with a big head on it? 'Cause if it is she'll really get off, know what I mean?"

"Like a doorknob," I said. "Let me put it this way: you won't be wanting a refund. She'll like what I give her."

The geek nodded some more. I was tired of the ugly face; and couldn't stand to look at the cocksucker for more than about three seconds at a time.

"There's something else . . ." he said.

"Anything really outrageous, I get more money."

"She likes to be spanked, you know? Likes to have her ass whipped . . . with a belt."

"No sweat, and no extra charge, if that's all."

"Yeah, that's it, only do it like you're her father. Say shit like: Daddy's little girl's been bad. Is Daddy's little girl gonna be good now, is she? Will you be good to Daddy? You got it, all that shit."

"I got you." It wasn't all that unusual. My ex had a father fixation. She'd been molested by him for years. Strange? You might say. Only in her case she not only enjoyed it, she had initiated it. Admitted as much. More than once while I'd be there pumping her, driving it home, while she was orgasming, she'd be moaning crap about her Daddy. I didn't give a fuck, made no difference, as long as she got off, was having a good time, and then gave me a great blow job. That wasn't what worried me, what my primary concern was was just how homely was this cunt of his—and would she be able to keep her face turned away from me, as long as the body was there. He'd said she took care of herself. He'd said a lot—and you learned never to believe what a punk tells you, especially a degenerate punk like the one next to me. The asshole had more.

"She won't want it in the ass. Last son of a bitch was rough on her. She's still sore from it."

I shrugged. The one I had been married to years before only let me have that butt a couple of times. It was off limits to all but one. You guessed it. Daddy had exclusivity. There's no denying: those had been the best fucks I'd ever got out of her. She'd been too big down there, you see? A big pussy.

"If it works out," the dork said, "I'd like to hire you again."

"Fair enough," I said, and reminded him what I'd said about catching anything. "I'll track you down, amigo—and I'll kick your ass."

He understood. We walked outside to his beater. Dash was caked with grime, cracked, and had many cigarette burns. Film dust so thick on the windshield and other windows, outside and in, you could hardly see out. There was a stench: cat urine or something, you couldn't ignore. Ashtray overflowed with butts. Both knobs on the radio missing. If his wife had all the money he claimed, why was the sissy driving a heap like this? I also wondered about the rest of the money I was promised. Would it materialize? Did it even exist? Been burned too often in too many dealings with punks like this not to think this way.

We drove west on Melrose for a while, then took Western south to Wilshire. At Cochran he turned right. Drove half a block, parked.

"It's just a block north of here," he said. "I'd drive you to the building—neighbors, you know. Nosy. Been doing this for about a year and a half now."

I didn't care for walking in the heat and LA haze, but if I wanted the rest of the money I had no choice.

"Later," I told the guy, and walked the distance.

It was a salmon-colored stucco building, bordering on orange, two stories, four apartments. Hardwood floors probably. The kind of place I couldn't afford these days because they were asking for over a thousand bucks to let you move in.

I climbed the steps to the second floor and found the apartment I was looking for. The door wasn't locked, like the guy said, and I pushed in. Went inside. Unlike the wagon, the place was clean. Not much furniture, but all very neat: expensive dining table in the center of the living room, lots of green plants hanging from the ceiling and by the windows, one facing the alley and one the street. High-end stereo and speakers. If I'd have had a truck I could have loaded the shit up and pawned it. Books on art; one or two novels by that Jong bitch, the Dyer asshole (self-help); more than a few volumes on the medical profession; albums by the Eagles, Led Zeppelin (that I didn't give two farts for);

Laura Nyro I didn't mind; some jazz, very little jazz. Jazz, on the other hand, I liked to drink beer to.

But I felt frustrated standing there and taking in the stereo. I could have kept the money I already had and carried the stereo and speakers out the door. I think I was beyond all that. Too much work, besides, I was interested in seeing what she actually looked like, maybe a nice big ass and a tight cunt, good and hairy. Maybe she knew how to really suck it. But I knew better than to let my hopes soar, because not many women knew what to do with it. My former shack job did, but it had taken months for me to teach her how—and then after all that someone else had ended up with it.

The bedroom was to my left, at the end of the hallway. I walked slowly, reached it. The bed was there, and she was on top of it, face down, like he said, and naked. Healthy body with the kind of big ass I could never get enough of. I liked women built like this. The legs looked good. She even had tits, but I couldn't tell exactly how big.

The legs were tied to the bed posts, as were the arms at the wrists and she began to put some movement into the thick blond patch of hair below her brown butt hole. Yeah, I liked the way that brown asshole looked, the womanly buttocks, hips. She knew I was in the room and was putting on the show. My cock was getting hard inside my trousers. Her butt rose up off the bed sheet just a little, just enough to give me a grander view of some of that fine *culo* and light hairs around it. There was a small wart or blemish just to the right of her asshole, but that didn't bother me at all. This was a woman who liked to tan herself, and the tan lines added to the excitement. My cock was ready, twitching and jerking.

I walked over to the bed and started licking her legs, the pussy, everywhere. I got my tongue in her butt crack and kept it there a long while, then moved out and down to the cunt lips. I flicked the clit and her movements increased; she was making muffled yelps; gasps, too. This was too good to be true. She must have had a face so ugly they had a hard time finding anyone who'd fuck her, without paying good money, like they were doing now. But that was all right, I was game.

I stopped what I'd been doing to get some air, then reached over for the leather belt hanging from a hat rack on the closet door on my right and did like the suitcase pimp asked, gave her a few licks across that healthy ass. She liked it, breathing hard. Moaned plenty. I was working up a sweat at this point, but a good sweat. You couldn't really call it work.

"Daddy's little girl's been bad. Daddy has to punish his little girl now."

My cock good and hard at this point, was twitching inside my shorts. I unzipped my fly and let it out for air. There it was: stiff, pointing straight up, wanting it.

I belted her a few more times, then dropped the belt, slid my cock up that juicy cunt and worked it for a while, was tempted to jam it in her asshole. I wanted the rest of my fee. Only thing that stopped me. It was tempting. The quickest way to get me to do something is to tell me that I can't. I'd been warned to keep clear of her rectum. It was not easy. I kept riding the pee hole.

Hell, had I known, I would have fucked the broad free of charge. I should be paying them, I thought, as I unloaded! It lasted; I held on firmly as it did and collapsed against her buttocks, needing my rest. After that my face slid down to where her butt was and I kept it buried for a while. Butt sniffer. That's me. I kissed the small of her back and moved up, toward her neck and face.

At this point I was curious what the broad looked like and casually pushed the blindfold back, away from her eyes—and that's when I got the shock of my life: she looked a lot like the woman I'd shacked with about eight years back, the one with the daddy fixation, the one I'd fallen so hard for, when things had been better, when I still had some get-up and go left in me, when I still thought I might get somewhere, end up a little better off than where I was: nowhere—because she had taken off with my grubstake and fingered me to the rollers.

I did a double take. *Shit; was it her? Couldn't be,* but then this other stuff added up: her father had always wanted her to be in the medical profession, and yes, the whole time we were together she had fought against his wishes and wanted to do other things (that must not have worked out too well for her). Her old man was a big shot coroner on the East Coast. Got busted with two of his assistants for stealing from the dead. It wasn't bad enough that he'd been having intercourse with his own daughter for years, but he was quite efficient at relieving stiffs of their valuables and did serious time for it. I would let someone else try and make sense out of it all. I didn't have a fucking clue.

It was then I started to laugh, really laugh. I had attempted to take my life when she left me, hired a divorce lawyer to serve me the papers behind bars with my money; she had used my money to hire a lawyer— and lookit now what she'd ended up with, a suitcase pimp who couldn't get it up, who had to go out and find her guys who would fuck her for money, spank her butt and give it to her.

Life; man, life was pretty fucked up.

Was it really her, though? She couldn't be the only chick attached to Daddy, the only female with a jonze for Papa. Where was the proof? Some ID? Photos? I looked around for framed photos, but it looked like they'd all been put away, out of sight. I looked around for a purse, to go through, but didn't see one. My pecker was hungry for more and

I felt like jamming cock in her mouth for a blow job to end the game with, top it off, but my curiosity got the best of me. Where the fuck were all the photos people normally have around the house? What about photo albums? Where were they?

I climbed out of bed, went in the living room. Didn't find any there, either. They made certain no one got their hands on a photo and possibly attempted to blackmail them later. Who knew? Clever, cautious and perverted. Was it my ex? What were the chances in a place of ten million-plus that this was her? I followed my groin's lead and walked back to the bed. Shoved my chubby in her mouth. Forced it down in there.

"Okay, Gretchen; suck it!"

She went to town with it, like I knew she would. No one else had ever come close. She'd had a patient teacher in Ziggy Popper. She licked it, then moved in and out on it so that it disappeared inside her needy mouth every time. This created even more of a turn on for me, the fact I had been pumping her hole with it before and now it was in her greedy, salivating mouth.

I felt the inside of her throat as she sucked it in, deep. It pissed me off just a bit, too; there was malice and a feeling of payback time, baby. After all, I'd been the one who had shown the patience to train her and now some other asshole was getting it on a regular basis. True enough, Daddy had been her original teacher, busted her cherry, but I came along and fine-tuned her skills in the art of blowing cock. This was my one chance to get back, get mine. Never came by to say hello when I was in the joint. I'd been pushing weed and a good deal of the money I'd made had been spent on her: new car, trips to Vegas and Reno, hairdos and clothes. Not to mention shoes; lots of shoes. I'd gone from selling used cars to selling weed—just to please her. Was always after me to make more money, more money. No matter how much I spent on her it was never enough. I was smart enough to stash close to two hundred Gs that I had planned on opening up my own car lot with: *Ziggy Popper's Pre-Owned Classic Autos.* Bitch discovered my hiding place, cleaned me out, then set me up for the sting. Undercover rollers got to her. Skank sang like a canary. Never mind that the guy I was buying the weed from was a pal of hers, had in fact, introduced me to him. Gabe Chihuahua. *Gabron* was more like it. Water on the brain since the age of two. Fat neck and head. Hunched over. Had a shunt inside his lopsided skull to control the pressure and prevent the melon from exploding. Many surgeries; dozens upon dozens of surgeries since childhood. Add a unibrow on top. Average height. Overweight by forty pounds. Add a slur to his speech. Not stupid, just sounded like it. In fact, smarter than me, because *he sang like a stoolie* himself to keep his ass out of stir, and mine in. Judge gave me seven years. Did a nickel in Q and released for good behavior. All I ever got from her while in the slam was divorce papers. Cut me loose like I was a turd she couldn't wait to flush away.

Gretchen Krull. It should have been spelled Cruel, if you ask me. Cruel. *With an upper case "C"—for Cunt.*

This is Ziggy Popper, who never forgets. Ziggy Popper harbors a grudge and believes in payback. If I ever got my hands on Chihuahua I'd yank that shunt right out of his retarded, water-on-the-brain noggin.

I untied one of her hands to help her along with what she was doing: she needed it to lay off with the tongue and lips for a while and just stroke, slide her hand up and back down to the base, rubbing all that saliva on it. She spit in her hand, hard, got plenty of saliva on it, then rubbed it this way over the knob. My God, this was too much! The head of my cock was just too goddamn sensitive! It was way too much. I couldn't hold back any longer, didn't want to! Jammed it so hard inside her throat I could feel her tonsils.

"SUCK CUM, BITCH! EAT CUM, GRETCHEN, YOU FUCKING HARLOT! YOU CUNT! ARGGGH!"

I rolled off. Was on my back. Too spent to utter a word, or make a sound. Just kept breathing, trying to collect myself, but I could hear her chuckling or giggling about something, damn proud of herself. Well, well, she had a right to be. It was then I heard a faint thumping sound or something, coming from the closet. From somewhere near, but I couldn't be sure, was too exhausted to lift my head.

"You hear that?"

"Hear what? I didn't hear anything."

"What's that noise, Gretchen?"

"You keep calling me Gretchen. That's not my name."

"All right, what's your name, bitch?"

"Don't call me bitch. My name is Cordelia."

"Cordelia, huh? Okay, bitch, play your game. 'Cause I don't really give a fart."

"I told you—"

"What I don't understand is how you could dump me for a loser like that. I mean, I always thought deep down you were a cunt, but a punk who writes poetry and can't even get it up?"

"You got paid. Now you can get the fuck out."

"I got two twenties coming."

"You need to leave."

"You kicking me out, Gretchen? Is that it? After what just happened?"

"You got paid, you got laid—now get your sorry fucking ass out of here before I dial 9-1-1! Get me!"

"I got more money coming."

"You got shit coming. You should be paying me."

I sat up, looked at her, and the more she talked the more I became convinced this was the heartless conniver who had left me for dead, left me in the joint to rot away like a vegetable. Never called once all the years I was stuck inside. Had no one else to help. She was all I had. I thought she gave a damn.

"They beat me in there, had me on meds: Prozac, some other shit—and you never stopped by to see me once, Gretchen. How could you be like that? You flew back to the East Coast every chance you got to visit Daddy in the joint. That's a five-hour flight—on my dime. Never once came by to see me even though it's no more than a sixty, sixty-five-minute plane ride up the coast."

"I don't know what you're even talking about. You keep calling me Gretchen. Are you fucked in the head, is that your problem?"

"I was beaten; I was raped, you ball-busting sack of snot!"

"Sounds like you need help," she said, reaching for the phone.

"Don't do that, Gretchen," I said, then kicked the receiver out of her hand. I straddled her. She threw a punch, hitting me in the nose that made it bleed. Blood dripped down. *"Where's my two hundred Gs, whore? You're no different from that thieving daddy of yours who ripped off the dead."*

"What the fuck are you talking about?"

"You can stop pretending. I remember all of it: worked out of the Chief Medical Examiner's Office. Busted for robbing the dead. Him and his two assistants."

"Wait a minute, mister—"

"You never, ever gave a shit, did you, cunt? A cunt through and through. All I ever meant to you was the jack I pulled in. User; you and Chihuahua! Users! Opportunists! You two set me up to get off the hook. Bet you never gave two turds about *Gabron*, either. Only sided with him because he brought in the green. Admit it. Where is the stoolie now? Where is he? Still dealing dope? Still on the loose with that shunt in his skull dealing weed and who knows what else? Why'd you have to backstab me? I didn't deserve to be ratted out like that!"

She attempted to throw another punch. I blocked that, then punched down hard, hitting her in the mouth. There was blood on her teeth. She screamed, attempted to. I had my hand over her mouth, to stifle it.

"Go ahead, bitch! Scream all you want! Ain't nobody gonna hear!"

I reached for the belt, had to let go of her mouth to do that, then started whacking her, all over: her ass and everywhere else. Fuck it. She had it coming. She kept screaming, then: *"ROY! ROY! HELP! GODDAMN YOU, ROY!"*

I grabbed the tube of lube and squeezed out plenty on her butt, then slid my middle finger deep inside her shitter, getting plenty of the lube in there. The situation, roughness and violence, had my adrenalin going and gave me a third boner. I got the head of my cock in there, watched her attempt to twist and turn to shake me off, to no avail, then I drove the rest of my woody in. I had my zucchini deep inside her. Goddamn right. It felt too incredible for words: warm and tight, tight, the way it should be, and intensified every stroke a thousand fold. I kept at it; didn't give a shit whose name she continued to scream or what any of it meant. If the suitcase pimp jumped me, I'd take care of his ass, too, beat him down, rob them both, take what I could.

"GET OUT HERE, YOU ASSHOLE! THIS COCKSUCKER IS HURTING ME, ROY!"

She was too exhausted to put up much of a struggle. I kept at it, liking it. *Payback time! Fuck yes!* Nobody does Ziggy Popper like that and gets away with it! *Nobody!* I heard a loud crash, a wooden partition, the closet door banged open, and the punk from the bar, her "husband," staggered down to the floor with a video camera in one hand and his wiener in the other. I withdrew, then jammed it inside her mouth and unloaded. The distraction was too much. Damn near ruined it for me. I jumped up, leaping off the bed.

"Mother-fucking perverts!" I yelled. Kicked the punk in the head and watched him reel back against the closet door. Then I stomped the video camera. Fucking deviant had been videotaping the whole thing through that two-way mirror in the door while stroking himself. I picked up what was left of the camcorder and flung it at the wall and watched it disintegrate. The punk was moaning, clutching his bleeding jaw. His pecker having gone soft by now. He yelled something like: *"Go for it! Get it!"* to her. She was reaching under the mattress with her right hand for something, maybe a piece; I suspected it was a piece. Knowing Gretchen, if it was a handgun they had hidden under there, she wouldn't hesitate to use it.

I was back at her end, letting her have it with the belt, across her face, tits and back, and the same across her thighs, buttocks. I didn't give a shit. The bitch was bawling now; both were crying. White trash losers. I reached under the mattress. There was a .357 Magnum there. Blue steel. Nice and shiny. Goddamn, they could have fixed it good for me. A *.357 Magnum.* She'd never been crazy about guns, never been exactly against them, either, but she had never been violent that way, although quite violent and abusive in an emotional way (and many other ways), like so many of her kind knew how to be and took great satisfaction in it.

As I held the Mag, admiring it, she clawed at me once more, my face, and I backhanded her with it, knocking her unconscious.

I walked over to the punk. He was sitting up, his back against the open closet door, his hands up, pleading. I aimed the Magnum at the motherfucker. Held it . . . just held it . . . Then did to him what I had to her: knocked him out. I think a tooth went flying somewhere, because I heard it land on the hardwood floor.

I went through his wallet, extracted the bills: about ninety bucks. Searched through the closet for her purse, found it: eighteen bucks, some credit cards that I didn't want, best way to get busted. Looked at her license. The name on it was: Delia Aviva Dombrowski.

Okay, so she wasn't Gretchen, but that made no difference to me. They were dirt, no matter how you looked at it. Fucking degenerates. Had it coming to them. Damn right. I went through the closet some more, to see if there was anything worth taking, worth carrying out the door—and noticed a bunch of video tapes in the corner, stacks of them. All had labels printed on them that said: *Mistress Mona's House of Pleasure & Pain*, etc. There was a color brochure, stills of the broad I had just knocked out, being whipped by men in black leather masks, etc., or else she was the one doing all the whipping, dressed in leather, with a cat o' nine tails or horse crop in her hand. High heels, black fishnets, garter belt, the whole number. They were customized tapes of her either pissing on johns or crapping on them—at times both. Dildos were shoved up rectums.

So they were in *show business*, making secret tapes of their sexual encounters with strange men and women and selling the shit without them knowing. Dirtbags is right. Fuck it all. I needed a smoke. Reached for the pack of Marlboro's in the pimp's pocket. There was some of his blood on the pack and I wiped it against his shirt. I lit up. His wristwatch looked interesting, until I took it off and had a closer look: a cheap-ass Timex. I jammed it in the punk's mouth and laughed when the punk coughed and spit it out. My balls itched. I wondered if the cocksucking, cum-addicted two-bit harlot had given me something in addition to the head? I was hungry and I was thirsty for a beer. But first

I needed to take a shit bad, went in the john, took a dump. Smoked up the cigarette while reading one of their colorful smut brochures. Not bad. Looked amusing even, and my dick was back to half-mast again, only I wasn't inclined to start pounding off; I needed to get the fuck out of the place.

I showered; I needed that after what I had just been through, needed to wash the stench off. Got into some clean clothes belonging to the woman's punk. I combed my hair in front of the medicine cabinet mirror. I thought to shave and apply some cologne. Gretchen used to go on and on about how her father had always been clean shaven and smelled good. Busted for ripping off the dead and doing time for it, but all she could talk about was how he was clean shaven and smelled good. Well, that's something no one could accuse me of: stealing from the dead. Smelling good? Sure. That was me. Like a rose. Felt like a new man. It didn't take much: clean clothes, shower and shave and some jack in your pocket—and you felt better about yourself. And I was sure to be feeling a whole lot better about myself once I unloaded the .357 for a hefty sum to some barfly on Alvarado Street. Just might pay that private detective down there, the Polack, a visit. What was his name? What the fuck was that name again? *Choo-Choo* something . . . B-B-Budzinski; Bednarski. No, no; *Buschitski*. That's it. *Choo-Choo Buschitski*. Give him a few bucks and see if he can locate the backstabber for me, track down *Gabron*, and maybe this ex-con can do a little payback number on them both.

I made myself a cheese sandwich on toasted rye bread and washed it down with a cold Bud. I grabbed another can of beer for the road, it was hot out there, then stepped outside. I crossed south on Wilshire and caught the east-bound bus to my neck of the woods. I got off at McArthur Park, crossed north, walked a few yards east to the nearest bar determined to take no less than two-fifty for the piece.

"Don't chu want it?"

I'd been with Yellow a couple of years by now. This was the early part of 1978. My weekly take hardly covered the rent on the furnished room I was living in in Hollywood. I'd started the gig in '76 intending it to be something temporary, to get me through until I could get a script sold to the studios or a short story to a slick mag like *Playboy* or *Penthouse* (or some such illusion). I had my heart set on directing, as I'd gone to some chicken-shit film school in Hollywood in the early part of the 70s for that on the GI Bill, only I was not getting anywhere at all. I didn't know anyone in the business and I hated schmoozing (because I simply could not stomach movie people). I thought: Well, the only way to really do it is to find the financing on your own. I had a low-budget screenplay ready and all I needed was money. Anytime a potential investor would climb in the cab I'd spring the idea on them. I got a lot of no's; in fact, they were mostly no's. The "yeses" turned out to be all bullshit. Fares would get in, hear out the idea, tell you they were ready and had money to invest just to pick your brain and waste your time. (Or else they were looking to fuck you, literally, as well as financially—and any other damn way they might think up.)

Just what did I expect in Hollywood? This was Tinseltown, after all. I realize that these days, years later, and the flick business—that should actually be called *The Fuck Business*; because usually that's what happens: you get fucked over—doesn't interest me to the extent that it did back then. I saw it as a lark, a joke, and the people in it, for the most part, a bunch of warped and corrupt flakes. It was nothing more than a big con game perpetrated on the gullible public. And movie stars? Actors? Showbiz celebrities in general I felt sorry for and never once bothered for an autograph, the few that I happened to meet in the cab. I left these self-absorbed, neurotic cases alone. As a youngster growing up in Chicago, my first interest, true and main interest, had always been books, fine prose. Books were my solace and salvation in time of need, my escape & way of coping with life. Books, the written word, fiction: from Dr. Seuss (as a kid) to Edgar Allan Poe, Jules Verne, Elie Wiesel, Bukowski, Eugene O'Neill, Hemingway and others. Involvement with movies in LA was something to pass the time, a way to make some money and get the hell out of the sickness that was/is Hollywood. But back in the 70s I was still naive in believing that there was a way for a nobody with my nothing, non-monied, non-connected background to be a part of.

I was cruising seventh and Alvarado in my hack when the guy flagged me down. He wore a rumpled dark suit, white shirt and red tie. He walked with a limp and claimed gangrene was eating away at his right foot and that they'd have to amputate pretty soon. He was Mexican-American, portly; and although he had that suit on, his appearance was sloppy at best. He was an attorney, he claimed, via a white business card he flashed before my eyes; and he had two things going that I didn't: a woman waiting at home for him and money in the bank. The two seemed inseparable: women and cash. This was LA. If you wanted the former, you had to have the latter. And when you had the latter, the former just kind of materialized on their own—as they always do when there's green round.

Lorenzo Brown (I think it used to be Gomez or something, and he'd changed it) was far from ethical, (what else was new in this place?) and he liked to sue people, particularly insurance companies.

I hadn't liked the guy, but thought: Maybe I can get him to back the film, if he's got the bankroll he claims, and maybe I can get the hell out of the cab business, out of LA, have some kind of normal life, a life at least: a car, a nice apartment away from skid row, a good woman to start a family with. I didn't need to be wealthy, I didn't need fame (there were enough dizzy types around these parts pursuing various illusions, fame being the biggest load of crap of all). Little things were satisfying to me, things that money couldn't buy.

I mentioned the film idea to my passenger.

"Hollywood?" said he. "The movies? Never thought about it."

"Would you consider it?" I asked.

"Sure; why not? There's lots of young cunt in the movie business."

"Oh yeah; and not only that, but you stand to make a few bucks."

"You should come up to my place in Echo Park—and we could discuss it over a couple of beers, amigo."

"You got it," said I.

He went on about what an expensive car he drove, the fact he owned a couple of apartment buildings and had knocked up about two dozen Latino women in the area. "The stupid bitches are all illegals; I ain't worried about them causing me trouble."

"What do you say to these women?" I asked, just to have something to say. "How do you get them interested?"

He laughed. "I promise to marry them," he said. "These dumb bitches; man, they don't know nothin'." He was chuckling and kept saying how ignorant the "wetbacks" were. The more he talked, the less I wanted any part of him. I simply disliked the cocksucker, that's all there was to it. Didn't like his looks. But I would go to his place, put up with the bullshit if there were some slight hope that he would finance this idea that I had for a flick. I was desperate to get out of the hack, desperate to hold on to what little remained of my sanity.

We were in Echo Park. It was late evening now. It was a nice two-story home we pulled up in front of. Quiet neighborhood. You had to be a lowlife grifter to get anywhere in this world, just about. I didn't have it. Wanting to play fair and straight, wanting to be up front and decent with people—I couldn't cut it. I didn't belong in this hellhole. What was I doing here? Why was I wasting my youth away in this warped environment? I was in my twenties back then, idealistic, as mentioned, but determined to prove to myself, if to no one else, that I was no quitter, that I had something to contribute, that I could be a "success." The arts meant everything to me; the arts made this unbearable existence bearable. I had no family to go to for support of any kind, no one to lean on, outside of several people I'd met at film school (who were veterans with similar hopes and dreams and just as broke as I was). I hadn't spoken to my parents or any of the other siblings (a younger brother and three sisters) in close to ten years. I had to prove to myself that I could go off on my own and accomplish something I could be proud of. However, there was no denying that I hated myself for having to deal with characters like this Lorenzo Brown asshole sitting in my backseat.

I parked the cab in front of the house. We climbed the stoop. He unlocked the front door, and we went in. It was dark inside until he flipped the light switch on the wall. His current lady was asleep upstairs and he kept calling her name.

"Tina? Tina?"

I told him I had to take a leak. He showed me to the john, and lingered. The hell kind of creep was this Lorenzo Brown anyway?

"Why don't you get the beer?" I muttered so I could relieve myself in peace. He left, calling the woman's name. I finished off, returned to the living room. I didn't like being here. The silly-ass crap one went through to make a dream happen. Well, if it got me out of the rut I was in and gave me a start as a filmmaker it would be worth it. Or would it?

He had two bottles of Bud sitting on the kitchen counter and was introducing me to a sleepy-eyed, dark-haired woman in a nightgown as she descended the stairs. She made the effort and got a brief smile going. I smiled back, and felt sorry for her. I didn't know her, anything about her, but I felt sorry for her. She was too good for the scumbag, too damn good. Even a mangy mutt would have been too good for him.

I swallowed beer and didn't pay much attention as he explained to her in Spanish why he had brought me home with him. Then he said something else to her that I didn't quite understand.

She went back up.

"What chu think?" he asked.

I nodded. "Okay."

"Shit," he said. "Better than okay. A lot better. For a guy like me."

I didn't disagree.

"She's twenty-three," he said, and laughed. "She'll do anything I ask."

I drank my beer.

"You want some of that?" he asked. "Huh? Want some?"

I shrugged, and asked for another beer.

"You know what beer does to some guys," he said. "Sure you want more?"

"Why not?"

He got the beer, and felt a need to remind me: "Some guys can't get it up when they drink."

We both looked up as she appeared at the top of the stairs wearing a practically transparent off-white shorter version of what she'd had on earlier, hair combed. She had cleaned her face and applied just the right amount of makeup. She looked pretty, but she seemed sad for some reason to me. She came down the steps, the smile more accessible; walked to the kitchen part of the setup and got the coffee pot going.

Lorenzo Brown talked on and on, how great she was in bed. "Juicy and tight. Got a magic tongue. Pure magic." He was chuckling at his own delivery, maybe the anticipation of what he thought was about to happen.

Any other time I might have been interested; she was sexy enough and actually good looking enough—but I didn't like it this way. I don't go to bed with a woman unless the feeling is mutual, and in this case it couldn't have been. I knew it wasn't. I looked like shit. I reeked of sweat and BO; I needed a shave and a good shower. And I glanced at her from time to time as she worked to appear busy so as not to keep from revealing how embarrassed she felt. I started feeling uneasy about it myself, and did my best to shift the conversation over to the production and what it would entail, although I knew there would be no backing, mainly because I was sure I didn't want any part of him, and also because he'd been stringing me along, had no intentions to invest, that was clear by now (not that I was sure *he had anything to invest*).

But he kept on about her, about sex; and it finally came out that he was impotent, had been for five years, and said he didn't know why. He'd gone to see a shrink about it and the "jive turkey" didn't know why either.

I wanted to make a suggestion that maybe the gangrene in his foot had gotten to either his nuts or his brain, but didn't.

She had her coffee mug in her hand and sat down in a chair, did her best to keep smiling and appear pleasant. None of this is your fault, I felt like saying to her; I have nothing against you personally.

"How much you want?" he finally said.

I looked at him. It was like a slap in the face, the final insult.

"I don't care about money, money is of no importance. She needs to get laid."

I didn't know what to say. Kept drinking my beer and shrugged.

"Don't be bashful," he said. "What do you think?"

"What about the film?" I suggested, to get off the subject.

He laughed. "Don't you want to fuck her?" Walked over to where she sat in the black leather chair. He lifted the hem of the nightgown and parted her thighs. She wasn't wearing panties, that I could tell. There was a lot of hair down there, dark, a nice patch of it. I love a woman with a hairy cunt; it's the biggest turn on. A big healthy womanly ass. And she had it. She brushed his hand away, but did it in such a way so as not to offend. She rose and found some soft playing music on the stereo. He followed after her, grabbing from behind and squeezing her tits. He had her facing him, and they slow-danced, with Lorenzo Brown doing what he could with that bum foot of his and she not being able to do much as she still held the coffee mug in her hand. He relieved her of the coffee mug, set it down on the kitchen counter and continued with the slow moves, running his hand down between her thighs and then up between the cheeks of her rear end. All the while he kept eyeing me and saying: *What do you think? Don't chu want it? Good pussy, man. Good pussy.*

"Good-looking lady," I believe I finally said. "That's for sure."

"That's all you got to say? Take your clothes off, man; come on."

I shook my head.

"What's a matter, amigo? You queer?"

"I don't think so."

"Not sure?'

"Some other time."

"What'sa matter with chu, man? I'll pay you. I'll just watch. I'll pay you—" and he went for his wallet, extracting some bills, and I didn't exactly see how much he held in his fist because I was already on my way out the door by then.

Birdman of Tucson

He'd just gotten rid of his tv and in trying to get used to the silence in his modest one-bedroom cribby, he thought he'd get a couple of birds. He'd had parakeets as a kid growing up and had always loved birds, any kind: large, small. He would have liked being able to afford a cockatoo, something along those lines, only his fixed budget dictated that he go for something more reasonable. He had a dog in his small front yard in this four-plex that he lived in, but the dog was an outdoor dog and he had been meaning to get a bird for a few years now. The timing was right, a singing little birdie in place of the tv he loathed. Television sitcoms, talk shows, game shows, entertainment shows, news shows he loathed with such a passion that he'd given away a practically brand-new color set. And he'd done this more than once in the past. Why buy tvs when you can't stand tv? Good question. He hadn't minded some of the programming: PBS, the occasional worthwhile film, the educational docs. Although it hardly made the rest of the tripe that was on there worthwhile.

So now the tv was gone and he thought a birdcage with a pet bird in it sitting atop the counter against the far wall couldn't be more appropriate.

He climbed on his bicycle and rode it the four miles out to the pet store. This was a large facility that also sold saddles, horse feed, pups, fish, cats, pot bellied pigs, etc. A rather wonderful facility for any animal lover to be inside of and browse. He did that for a bit, to acquaint himself with the place. Noticed the aviary room to the side on the right as you entered. He went in. The pet shop owner had all sorts of birds in there: large four-hundred, five-hundred and six-hundred dollar parrots. He saw a couple of yellow ones at $250 a piece. Too much for his budget. The parakeets, on the other hand, were too young to be sold and the woman couldn't tell what their sex was just yet. He was hoping to get a male and a female.

He let her talk him into picking up a couple of finches at $11.95 each. She had to go tend to something in back. Said she would be right out. While she did that, the man looked about the store, trying to figure out what else he might need. He could not believe he was actually taking the time to do this. He'd wanted to get a bird or two for years but the opportunity was never there, always too busy doing something or other.

After a while, he could hear the lady back in the bird room, talking to a middle-aged couple. The pet shop owner was holding a small brown paper sack with something in it. Small bird? He wasn't sure. He could hear her say: "I have a man who was looking to buy parakeets who might be interested in the love bird."

She looked up when he stepped into the bird room. "A lady just now brought this bird in that I can let you have for free, if you're interested."

"I guess so, sure."

"You weren't really interested in the finches, were you?"

"No," he said, "not really; but I was interested in taking a couple if that was all I could get."

"I won't charge you anything for this bird," she said.

"What kind is it?" he asked.

"Love bird," she said.

He wondered if he might take a peek inside the bag.

"Sure," she said, and cautiously unfolded the top of the bag. The man leaned over and caught a glimpse of a green parrot. It was then the gray-haired man said: "If you don't want her, I'll take her. I've never had any trouble with any of the birds I got here."

"Sure, I'll take the bird," the man without the tv said. The man with the gray hair turned to the shop owner asking for certain birds and made it clear that if she didn't get them pretty soon he would go to her competitor, etc. "I may have to go to California to get them," she said.

"All right then. We'll see you."

The couple left. The pet shop owner helped the man pick out certain things he would need for the love bird: bird seed, cuttle bone, a toy bell. It totaled sixteen dollars something. He didn't need to buy a cage since he already had one.

When it came time to take the bird out of the bag, she had a green net to do it with. It was a blue/green/orange and red parrot twice the size of your average parakeet and feisty to boot. The bird continuously bit the woman; it was a battle. A female clerk came up to assist with a pair of scissors. They were going to clip the bird's wings.

"Is that necessary?" asked the man, not knowing much about birds after all.

"Oh yeah," she said, "otherwise she could hurt herself while flapping her wings inside the cage." She added: "It doesn't hurt them at all and the wings'll grow back."

They did that. It was a task, but the woman managed it. You could see the pet shop owner wince each and every time the bird bit her hand.

"Is she hurting you?" the assistant asked.

"Oh yes," said the owner of the store.

Finally the deed was done and the bird was placed inside a small cardboard box and the flaps closed. The man paid for the items with his credit card. Shook the woman's hand and said: "You're very nice. Thank you."

"Why, you're very welcome."

He carried the small box with his new pet outside to where he had his bicycle locked up and rode home. One thing he noticed while hurrying to ready the cage for the bird (filling seed tray, water tray, and doing his best to shorten the chain on the bell in order to fit inside the cage that may have been a mite small for this bird) was how not only noisy but feisty the bird was. He then noticed that the bird had chewed away with its beak enough of an opening in the cardboard to poke its head through. That's one tough "love bird," he thought.

He had the cage on the kitchen table, the box next to it. Cut away the tape the woman had used to seal the flaps with and held it up against the opening in the cage. It took some doing but he managed to coax the bird to get in the cage.

The bird liked reggae music and chirped to it happily. Sunday morning was a sunny day with other birds chirping nearby in trees, etc. He had to go do his laundry but thought he might leave the birdcage atop the barbecue in his front yard in order for the parrot to enjoy the sunshine and other birds.

When he got back, he brought the bird inside, opened the cage door for the parrot to get out if it wanted to. It took the bird a good fifteen minutes to make up its mind. This bird, that he did not have a name for yet, was not a friendly bird. He did not just play with the bell, he attacked it. He did not just dip into the seed tray, he kicked it around with his beak, knocking plenty down on the living room carpeting. Instead of drinking water from the water tray, he got in there and thrashed around. He was determined to tear the cage apart, it seemed, if he could. None of this the new bird owner minded, with the exception of the bird darting at his fingers, hand, whenever he attempted to replace seeds or make adjustments with the clips holding a slice of apple or cucumber.

Well, in time, he thought; in time, this bird and I will become pals.

It soon became evident, there was no denying it, this was one pissed off bird. Often times he was busy reconstructing his missing wings from the newsprint on the floor of his cage, or else cutting up paper outside his cage, the times he was allowed outside the cage, into wing-like shapes and attaching them to what remained of his shortened wings in back. He wanted his wings back so he could fly about. As it was, he was only able to make short hops from the counter against the wall where the cage sat, down to either the sofa or floor. The counter was but three feet off the floor, but still too high for the parrot to make from the floor. The man wanted to adjust the mirror affixed to the cage (he had it there for the bird to play with; and in fact, the bird had been convinced there was another of its ilk there) and the bird made an effort to fly up from the floor to the counter and came up short by a foot, banged its head against the wood door below and dropped to the carpet.

The man thought about the bird, how to improve its situation. He would buy a bigger cage, new water and seed trays, etc.

While buying groceries for himself at the market the next day, he'd picked up a fruit and seed stick for the bird, a new water tray. The problem was every time he got his hand inside the cage, he got pecked for his troubles. He would refill the water and the bird would go after his hand, biting him, never breaking the skin, but the bites were sharp nevertheless, sharp and stung plenty.

Well, okay; it's a new relationship we're beginning here. These things take time. He'd tried using cotton gloves whenever sticking his hand inside the cage but the gloves made it all the more cumbersome. There just was not enough room inside the cage. It was when he had refilled the seed tray and attempted to hook it back up did the bird go after him and viciously enough this time with that honed beak that it caused the man to react and knock over the seed tray and water tray both, spilling the contents on the birdcage floor as well as outside the cage. This thoroughly irritated the man.

"I'm trying to feed you, you little shit, and this is how you thank me. No wonder they gave you away. No wonder the lady who gave you up didn't want you. Asshole is what you are. *Yeah you.*"

He sprayed the bird with saliva as the only way he could get back at it and not cause it any real harm. But he was truly pissed at the bird, at the mess it caused, at the woman who owned the pet store and that white-haired idiot who kept insisting: *"I've never had any trouble with birds I got from here, only other places."*

"I've got a psycho parrot on my hands," said the man to himself. "A real Norman Bates; better yet: Mike Tyson. That's it, the boxer who bit off a chunk of Holyfield's ear that time. *Tyson.* Got yourself a moniker, tough guy."

He slipped the gloves on, got one hand inside the cage, removed the perch bars, then grabbed at the bird, not that it was easy, but he got his hand on the goddamn bird. He was going to talk to it, spray more saliva on it if need be, if that was what it took to teach it a lesson. He held it in his right fist and all the while the bird attempted and did succeed in wrapping its beak around the wool cloth of the brown glove. *Son of a bitch. This bird is just too goddamn mean.* What gives? Do I need this? He felt it struggling inside his grasp, all the while doing its best to bite him. They were strong bites, the beak sharp, making some cuts in the cloth.

"Settle down, asshole." The bird wouldn't hear of it. "Nobody's trying to hurt you here. I'm on your side."

The bird paid no attention and wanted nothing short of the man's blood. After a few minutes of this, there was nothing else to do but place it back inside the cage. He did not close the gate to the cage. "Just to show you there ain't no hard feelings. You want to stay inside, you can stay. Want to get out—get out. Up to you."

The bird remained inside, its chest pounding, its back turned to the man.

"Fuck you then," the man hissed at the bird, walked away. He was tired of this bird and its bullshit and he had better things to do. He reached in his closet for the stack of skin mags on the top shelf. But that bored him. He had the radio tuned to a jazz station. He thought about the way this latest attempt to liven his apartment had pretty much backfired on him. This was a nasty bird, no doubt about it; dark green where it was green and just a nasty disposition.

"I'm taking you back, sucker," he muttered to himself. "And I'm buying a couple of parakeets, like I intended all along. Lady said the bird was *free*. Hell; ain't nothing free in this cockamamie world. Nosireebob. Free my ass."

He walked to the john, took a leak, washed his hands. Glanced up at the forty-seven-year-old grizzled face that stared back. "You don't need no fucking bird, Jack. What you need is a woman, a woman. It's been too long, too long . . . A little singing birdie ain't going to fill that void. You need a woman to hold and hold and share laughter with, do things with; a real live human being and not some bird angry at the world."

Funny, that was what he'd found interesting about the bird in the beginning: the anger, feistiness. He could relate since this was the way he'd been most of his life, fucked childhood and whatnot. Yes, he'd been one anti-social, bitter, angry muther up until the age of forty. And for years he'd thought about getting a bird or two and now that he had a bird, the wrong bird, the anger was something he could do without. He'd had enough of that. He was finally at long last at peace with his past. History was something you couldn't do anything about. You had to go on, move forward. Be grateful for what one had and he was.

Fuck it. He would return the bird next weekend. This was Monday. Four days to go. All he had to do was keep his hand out of the cage, ignore the damn thing. Feed it, of course, with a glove on, but stay away from it otherwise.

He stretched out on the bed. He was okay now, over the initial anger of it, at the way the bird had attacked him. Really, I've never been happier in my whole life, never more content, with one exception: soul mate; but that could still happen. There was time. He didn't fret that part of it anymore. And *that* he considered quite a success in attitude and the way he approached life these days.

The bird? The bird would be dealt with soon enough. The evil little bastard would have to go. The word *evil* was appropriate here. Quite.

He recalled watching *20/20*, a tv show on this very subject a while back. In Australia, goats and sheep were being killed by the dozens by some type of creature, a chupacabra type of beast that had a way of attacking the animals from behind and cutting their necks and leaving them to bleed to death. Experts were brought in. It was baffling. They couldn't figure it out. Ranchers were up in arms: the slaughter was taking its toll. And it always took place under cover of night: many goats and sheep left to bleed to death.

There were no other hints or clues that suggested who was responsible until infrared vid cameras were set up to capture the culprit and/or culprits behind the mindless slaughter. To the shock and surprise of many, the green parrots, so-called *"love birds,"* were the guilty party. Hundreds or maybe even thousands would converge on the helpless farm animals who were too dumb to defend themselves and shake the birds off, hop on their back and peck away at the neck region until a large-enough cut was created for blood to seep out. The love birds were causing the senseless murder of valuable ranch animals on a grand scale and did so simply because they were *inherently venal and malicious . . .* and this is what the pet shop owner had given him for a pet: a malevolent and destructive little warbler that didn't warble.

With this in mind, the man set the clock radio that he had tuned to the oldies station to go off at 6:00 a.m. It was 9:48 p.m. presently. He took a deep breath, exhaled, closed his eyes, slept.

When next he awoke, it was to sharp, stinging pain, a wetness round his eyes, as the parrot pecked away at them. He swiped at the bird. Heard it screech. Hit the wall. The man staggered in the dark to seek out the light switch, flicked it—but still could not see. *God, no.* He rubbed gently at the surrounding area of his eyes. Nothing but a type of moisture. *Blood?* Staggered into the bathroom. Flicked the light switch. For more of the same. Found the medicine cabinet with his fingers—but could not see a thing. *The bird, the fucking bird had eaten away his eyeballs; rendered him totally blind!* But how was that possible?

He'd left it in its cage with the gate closed. How could the motherfucker have gotten out? It made no sense. And it was baffling.

It was then he jerked his head hard enough to snap out of the nightmare. Sat up. Waited for his eyes to focus and did. Could make things out in the dark from the front patio light he always left on before turning in for the night. He rose, turned on the bedroom light. He walked over to the birdcage in the living room, lifted the flannel shirt he'd left draped over the cage. The parrot was perched quietly on the plastic clip.

The next day after coming home from work, he carried the cage outside to the patio to let the bird have some sunlight, and as the man turned his head briefly, his hand on the cage, the bird attacked his finger, biting him hard, drawing blood. He cursed, pissed as hell, took the bird inside, grabbed a plastic ruler and whacked the cage a few times, making the bird jump, scaring it.

What was he going to do about this goddamn, vicious bird? This bloodthirsty fucking bird? The following day didn't fair any better. The man arrived home to find the water tray on the bird cage floor. The next day the same thing. He carried the cage outside, to the front yard, opened the cage door, went back inside the apartment. A few minutes later he took a look outside and saw the bird pecking away at the tread on his rear bicycle tire. He waved his arm and the bird hopped off, landing in the weeds in the yard. Fuck it.

"You want to be free? There you are, fucker. Fly away. Go for it. See how long you last."

The bird, looking quite beautiful now in the sunlight, the green and blue and red on top of its head bright in the afternoon Tucson sunlight. The man's dog was but ten feet away, perhaps about to go after the bird. Although normally a harmless dog with a quiet demeanor, the man couldn't be sure and his conscience got the best of him and made the effort to chase the bird back inside the cage. The dog got closer and more than once the man had to stop, point his finger at the dog and order it not to move. The dog, being a good dog, obeyed. It took a few minutes of chasing the bird back and forth across the small yard, among the dog crap—the man had to be careful not to step in the dry dog poop—and eventually was able to guide the bird back inside the cage; carried it back indoors.

At his warehouse job where he was employed as a shipping clerk, the new bird owner appeared preoccupied, stressed out. No doubt about it: problems with the bird was taking its toll on his otherwise generally positive outlook on life. *Would he have to return the bird back to the pet shop?* He'd liked the bird's feistiness, in spite of the attacks; and yet the senseless assaults on his being, his kindness, was stressing him out and bringing out the worst in him. This was no good, no good at all—not when he finally in his mid-forties was content and at peace with his existence, his lot. He didn't like being angry. It made no sense to let a little "love bird" put him through this.

What to do?

Each and every day he dreaded going home, reaching his abode from fear what he might discover, the mess the bird had caused. He reached his abode later that day. Fear had been justified. Water tray had been turned over again and was on the birdcage floor, mirror chewed up. Newsprint in strips on the bottom of the cage, bird seed strewn about on the countertop.

No way around it: bird would have to go. The man had been too angry lately and all due to the bird. He got into the gloves, reached inside to grab the bird. It put up a fierce battle, and he could hear its beak rattling, it feared him that much. *You fearing me? Me? I never attacked you, never bit you, drawing blood.* "You drew first blood, sucker!"

The bird chirped, screaming for help as though its end were near. Gimme a break, thought the man.

"Nobody's going to harm you. Although I'd like to twist your scrawny little neck, asshole," the man hissed.

He grabbed it, withdrew it from the cage while the bird worked away with its beak, doing its furious best to bite through the cloth of his glove. The man had no choice but to clamp the beak down with his left hand, and while attempting to do this, the bird bit into his index finger, through the cloth, same spot as before, drawing blood.

"That does it, you son of a bitch! You're going back! Cocksucker! I've had it!"

He held its beak down with thumb and index finger, while the rest of the bird's body he held in his right hand. The bird made what sounded like desperate sounds for help, bird yelps. *"No one's going to hurt you, asshole, although . . . Fuck it. I've had it."*

He placed the bird inside the cardboard box, taped the flaps down, making certain to leave a partial opening on top for air to get through.

He climbed on his bicycle, holding the bird in its box in one hand, while steering the handlebar with the other, and rode the four miles this way to the pet shop at the corner of Dodge and Campbell. He was relieved it had finally come to this. To hell with it. He'd tried his best, treated the bird with every kindness, spent about thirty dollars in all on that mirror, fruit sticks, bell, food and water trays, cuttle bone, sand perch covers (that's how the little fucker had been able to sharpen his beak so well), bird gravel he'd sprinkled the cage floor with. All that hadn't been enough for the angry cocksucker. Fuck him. He'd tried.

He locked the bike up outside the pet store, picked the box up, went in. Explained why he was bringing the bird back.

"So, he's an unhappy little camper," the woman said.

"I wouldn't give him to anyone with kids. He just might peck their eyes out."

He walked outside, mounted the bicycle, and while pedaling back to his place he thought he should have felt better than he did. He couldn't figure it. The bird was a problem and he'd gotten rid of the problem. He'd tolerated its bullshit for over a month: fed it, took care of it, and the bird, Tyson, had paid him by biting him repeatedly. Yeah, but if he were honest with himself, he couldn't deny the connection: he'd been able to relate. He'd spent most of *his* existence full of rage . . . something that was easy to relate to about the bird . . . And now it was gone, out of his life.

He should have been happier than he was; should be glad, truly relieved . . . but he wasn't. He might have been able to establish a bond with the little bastard if he'd given it more time. It might have happened. Instead he'd given up on the bird so easily, so easily . . .

The next day on the job he spoke hardly two words to his fellow coworkers, which was atypical of him, and could sense they were aware of it. He missed the bird, that day and the next. Missed the fucker. He could have been more patient. All the people, the few true friends he'd had in his life, had all been patient with him all those years he'd had his ups and downs. He'd called it quits too easily, given up too fast. The bird was but a year old. Young, young. They live to be twenty years old, the woman at the pet shop had told him. Yeah, and he'd given up. *Shit!*

The Devil Liked That

He'd been drunk for eighteen months now, stayed in his room and drank in the dark. Would only venture outside to buy more booze, maybe a loaf of bread, can of soup, chips. He was on his last leg and he knew it; he was ready. Soon he would walk the block or so to Wilshire, ride the elevator to the top of the office building and take that dive. He was through. His savings all but gone. What little he'd been able to save as a day laborer painting apartments, shampooing carpets, was down to nearly nothing. She had ended up with the car, dog, the trailer—sold the trailer, and taken off for Vegas with a tall, dark and handsome type. The way it always went. They always did that to you, they always did. And he had remained in the fleabag, killing roaches and spiders, masturbating, shitting and pissing, vomiting and more vomiting, crying. It didn't make much sense; at thirty-five he was ready to call it quits: no more—no more bullshit. This is it, man. He jumped in the chair when the phone rang, dropping the bottle, spilling beer over his stained shorts and worn carpet.

He picked up the receiver and didn't say anything.

"Reuben?" It was a husky male voice. "Reuben Belcrest?"

Who the hell can it be? he wondered. After a lengthy pause, he said: "Yeah?"

"Is this Reuben?"

"Yes."

"Listen, I can help you, man. I know all about your situation."

"What're you talking about? Who are you?" Reuben knew it couldn't have been the desk clerk; the wino would have been sacked out this late at night.

"I know your woman left you; I know you're planning on ending it. You don't think there's any point in going on—"

"Who the fuck are you?" Then it occurred to him it might be the FBI, but why? Maybe LAPD. Why? What'd he do? Some kind of frame-up.

"Who are you?" he said again.

"Please don't hang up on me when I tell you. Promise you'll hear me out first?"

Reuben hesitated, then nodded to himself. "You got it."

"Your woman's name is Marcy. You split up eighteen months ago, or rather *she* wanted out. You came close to buying a handgun and killing her and her new boyfriend. You haven't worked in just as long. You're a musician by profession, albeit not a very good one. You were able to make a living—not star material, but you paid the bills. You also do odd jobs: landscaping, repairing fences, painting apartments."

The man was right. Reuben listened.

Then the voice said: "I'm a friend who'd like to help, Reuben. I can get her back for you. I can do that."

"How?"

"I can, Reuben. I've done it before. I've got proof."

"I don't understand. Who are you, man? This the FBI? What'd you want?"

"I'd like to come and talk—"

"Tell you the truth . . . I'm not up to it at the moment—"

"I've got a fifth of good scotch here."

"LAPD, right?"

"Wrong, Reuben. Can I come up?"

"Give me fifteen minutes."

"Fine. See you in fifteen, Reuben."

Reuben lowered the receiver into the cradle and lingered a moment. The hell was going on? The guy knew everything. Someone had kept an eye on him, someone out there. *Who? And why? Was it Marcy?* Maybe she finally realized what the breakup was doing to him, killing him, slowly squeezing the lifeblood out of him. But he knew better. Things like that only happened in the movies, the fucking bullshit Hollywood movies. In real life, once they were tired of you, they left you crawling, begging, whimpering. Laughed as you slowly withered away and died.

Reuben got into the beer-stained trousers, the torn shirt, made it to the bathroom down the hall, slapped water on his face, rinsed his mouth a couple of times, brushed his hair back with his hands. He noticed a wart on his bruised forehead. A wart? A fucking wart. He'd never had a wart in his life. Where the hell did that come from? Forget the wart. You can always slice it off with a razor blade later.

God, what a mess, he thought. Even if she ever did return he'd never be able to face her. He was a wreck and knew he'd never be able to look the way he once did.

He took a piss in the stopped up crapper full of some wino's turds and walked back to his room. He was nervous now, too much so. Paranoia. The voice over the phone had made him edgy, the fear was creeping back in; the fear. He'd been okay up to now—but they knew about him, they knew.

He turned on the lamp on the dresser. Stood before the framed color snapshots of Marcy. He looked at the photos and his eyes watered. God . . . He shook his head. It wasn't fair, it wasn't right. He felt his guts churning and hurried down the hall to the restroom, but the door was locked and he puked his guts out just outside it.

He made it back to his room, got a beer out and waited for the man to knock on his door. When it did happen it startled him just the same. He turned on the overhead light. It was weak, like the lamp on the battered dresser. They charged as much as they could and gave you as little as they were able to get away with. He opened the door.

The man was well over six feet, impeccably dressed in a blue-gray three-piece suit, maybe in his early forties. Just a touch of silver in his neatly clipped sideburns. A good-looking, healthy son of a bitch. Law enforcement material.

"May I come in?" the man said.

"Suit yourself," Reuben said, and returned to his ragged chair with the cotton stuffing coming out at the seams. The man pulled the scotch out of the brown paper sack he'd been carrying it in.

"I gotta wait a while," Reuben said, eyeing the bottle. "Got cramps in my guts right now. Should wait."

"It's yours," the man said. "I just wanted to talk anyway, let you hear my proposition."

"How about some ID," Reuben inquired. "Not that I give a shit. Just curious, know what I mean?"

The man smiled, shook his head. "I'm not the police, and I'm not the FBI, nothing like that—"

At this point Reuben didn't give a damn what the guy was: mafia, bill collector, the Good Humor man.

"The fucking suspense is killing me. What do you want?"

"That's your girl Marcy, isn't it?" the man said, as he walked over to the dresser.

"How do you know so much about me?"

The man only smiled, picked up one of the framed five-by-seven photos, held it in his hand, then faced it toward Reuben.

"Good-looking woman," the man said.

Reuben didn't say anything. Looked at his baby, looked. "Why don't you put the fucking picture down."

It was then the photo came alive. It was like a miniature tv screen. His Marcy was smiling, waving to him; *she was waving.* Reuben rubbed his eyes, stared. There she was: waving. He rubbed them again, shut them tight, slapped himself a few times. God, what's going on? Hypnotism, that's what's happened. The son of a bitch knows hypnosis. No, no, not even hypnosis could do that. It was the booze, the booze and other things had finally fried his brain, kicked his ass senseless, finally.

"Relax, Reuben," the man said. "You're not seeing things . . . believe me, you're not. She's waving, your lady is waving to you; she's smiling, glad to see you. . . ."

Reuben opened his eyes, looked at the man, returned his gaze to his beautiful Marcy.

"She wants to talk to you, Reuben. Listen. . . ."

"Hi, honey," It *was* her. She was talking to him, she was alive in that picture. "I miss you, Reuben honey. I can't tell you how bad I feel about what happened. That other guy was a creep. I don't even know why I left with him, honey. You're the one I love. I'll always love you, my darling Reuben. I just needed to get away for a while. I'd never been with anyone else. *Could you ever forgive me, Reuben? Please?*"

I'm *seeing things,* Reuben concluded. I don't care—I'm seeing things. There is no other explanation. I'm seeing and hearing things— this whole fucking thing—I'm dreaming. Gotta be.

"No," the man said. "You're not dreaming, Reuben. This is actually happening. Here and now. All of it."

The guy was reading his mind. Reuben rose to his feet. "Who the fuck are you, man? *Who are you?*" Reuben paced the room: once, twice, three times. Leaned in and grabbed the guy by the lapels. *"For the last goddamn time—"*

The man lost none of his composure, none of the self-assurance he had shown throughout, and said: "I'm the Devil."

"Mister, I'm at the end of my rope!"

It was then the man's skin began to turn a pinkish color until it was finally red, a flaming red. There were small flames in his eyes, coming out of his nose, mouth, ears. There was no suit there, just tiny crimson flames covered his entire body. Reuben let go that instant, as his hands had been partially burned already. Reuben dropped back in the chair, squeezing his skull. *God . . . what's happening here?* Maybe if he shut his eyes tight enough. Could it be he'd imagined it all? Hallucinated all of it? D.T.s? Gotta be. *Holly shit, I'm fucked up.* There's no hope.

When next he opened his eyes, the guy was still there, no longer covered in flame, but there, the neatly pressed suit intact as was the look of confidence. The Devil apologized for having taken that step, but had resorted to it to prove he was the genuine article.

"You're not imagining anything, Reuben. I can read your mind, I know what you're thinking."

Reuben looked up.

The Devil nodded.

"Everything. Now then, let's get down to it: you want your Marcy back. An easy enough task to accomplish on my part. All it takes is a bit of mental suggestion. In fact, she needs you right now so bad she's hurting."

Reuben didn't say anything. It wouldn't have made any difference. He would let it play out, let things happen.

"You can have your Marcy in return for a little favor first I'd like to ask of you." The man cleared his throat.

"I'll do anything," Reuben said. "You must know that by now."

The Devil grinning, nodded. "Right. Of course." Then pausing, added: "That roof you were thinking of jumping from . . ."

"Yeah . . ."

"I'd like you to do that, not jump of course, I wouldn't want you to jump—with your Marcy back at your side there wouldn't be any reason for you to do a dumb thing like that—"

"Get to the point, please."

"I'd like you to go up there, and walk along the ledge, just walk, nothing more."

"That's it? Go up to the top of the office building and take a stroll on the ledge. What for?"

"It's not important. Agreed?"

"Wait a minute. You don't want me to jump?"

The Devil chuckled. "No, of course not. I want to bring you two back together. You belong together. You want her and you shall have her."

"And you're doing this out of the goodness of your heart. Hell, you don't have a heart. What am I saying?"

The Devil kept chuckling.

"Hey, what am I supposed to think? I'm confused, man. You got me confused. You're the Devil, right? You say you're the Devil. Okay. Fine. Maybe you are."

"Take my word for it. I am."

"Okay, you are. Well, from what I heard, man, you don't go around doing good deeds, period. Am I getting across?"

The Devil nodded.

"I want to know why you want me to take that walk—"

The Devil shrugged. "What difference would it make to you? You're willing to do it. That's all that matters here."

"Yeah, right. You're just doing it to give the lunch hour crowd something to talk about when they return to work."

"All right, I'll level with you. There won't be a wind, I'll personally see to that, and no one will push you off, either, nothing like that. But there will be a suicide note, one that you will write. That's it."

"I need a beer," Reuben said. Got one out of the mini fridge. And as he did, he said to himself: God, I know I've never been all that religious. You got to get me out of this. Make this whole thing disappear.

"Do you want me to disappear, Reuben?"

Reuben was startled once again. "I keep forgetting: you read minds; the genuine article." He sighed, plopped back down in the chair, pulled on the bottle. "Where were we?"

"The suicide note," the Devil said.

"You don't want me to jump, but you want a sample of my handwriting."

"Here's why. It may sound a bit complicated, but it's all very simple actually: I'm doing it to prove a point to a colleague—"

"Colleague?"

"Yes. That's all. To prove a point."

"And what point is that, may I ask?"

"Simply that love is a sham, never works, was never meant to work. That love is a joke, a sad and often harmful joke, but a joke—perhaps that there is no such thing as love at all."

"If you're so against it, why are you bringing us together?"

"I told you—I could use a favor."

"Why me?"

"You seem to need it right now more than anyone; help, that is. I figured you would be more eager than most right now to go along with my little plan."

"How does a suicide note prove anything? It won't work."

"I conjure up a fake image of you dropping to the sidewalk, splattering in gory detail, the suicide note is found on your body, etcetera."

"You've lost me. If I'm really not dead—how does that prove anything? Huh?"

"You remain out of sight for a while—you and your Marcy."

The Devil withdrew the contract from an inside pocket. He held a fountain pen in his hand. He handed them both to Reuben.

"Okay," Reuben said. "But I want to see Marcy first. In the flesh. I have to make sure she still wants me. . . ."

"No problem."

"And I want *you* to sign a statement as well, that nothing happens to me; I don't get killed or hurt in any way. . . ."

"All right. . . ."

"That Marcy and I stay together forever . . . that we continue to love each other . . . take good care of one another. . . ."

"You got it, Reuben. Let's see your statement."

"I want to see Marcy first."

"She's at the Hollywood Greyhound waiting for you—"

"How'd she know I was coming?" Then he remembered: "Right. Mental suggestion."

"Exactly."

"But how did she know that I knew she was coming back?"

"I talked to her, Reuben. I simply told her I was a friend of yours, someone who had bumped into you, found out the kind of pain you were in, etc. What do you say?"

"All right," Reuben said. "You got a car?"

The Devil nodded, dangling a set of car keys in front of his face. He tossed the keys to Reuben. "If everything works out the way I planned, I may just let you have the car."

"Gimme a second here to clean up," Reuben said. Grabbed another pair of pants and a shirt out of the closet, a halfway decent towel, socks, a pair of shorts that were a little cleaner than the ones he was wearing and hurried down the hall to the restroom.

The door was locked. One of the other tenants was in there puking his guts out. "Your room's got a sink in it! Puke in your room! What the hell?" Reuben pounded on the door and continued pounding until the old guy staggered out of there, wiping vomit from his mouth and calling Reuben an ill-mannered cocksucker. Reuben went in, locked the door behind him, stripped down and dampened a corner of the towel and washed his genitals, under his arms. Held the towel under the spigot, wrung it out, got to his face and realized he needed a shave badly.

He dressed quickly, ran back to his room, grabbed his shaving gear and rushed back to the restroom, and shaved. He combed his hair, had a long look in the cracked mirror: it was an improvement. Yessir, he looked a little better. He returned to his room and told the Devil he was ready.

"Let's go," Reuben said.

The Devil held the contract in his hand. "How about we get this out of the way?"

"No chance," Reuben said. "You agreed."

The Devil nodded, and they walked outside to the car. Reuben's eyes were about to pop out of his head when he saw the car, a green 1968 Mustang. Marcy's favorite. She had always wanted a car like this. God, and the car might be his, too. And he'd give it to her. Reuben turned the key in the ignition, the Devil sat in the back. "It's quite all right," the Devil said. "I'll be invisible the whole time, so as not to ruin your reunion."

"Thanks," Reuben said, pulling away from the curb. He was excited for sure, more than excited, and yet felt funny, uneasy, something wasn't right, just wasn't right. It was too easy. Things didn't happen this way, not to a guy like him, never. He had begged and pleaded with her for so many weeks and months just to give them another chance and it hadn't worked, had threatened suicide and nothing had worked, and now it seemed to be falling into place just like that. She won't be there, Reuben thought; it's not possible. Okay, he's got me convinced he's the Devil, that's as far as it goes. It won't work out, can't. He doesn't want me to jump, just walk, just walk. . . . What kind of sense did it make?

The Devil cleared his throat from the backseat and said: "If you'd like to jump, that's all right, too, Reuben."

"Shit. I keep forgetting. Look, your explanation just doesn't cut it. I'll go along with you, still. . . ."

"Witnesses see you dive; there's the suicide note, publicity, headlines: the *Herald* and the *Times* and some other major papers across the country: JUMPER LEAPS TO HIS DEATH FOR LOVE or some such nonsense. But it will work, it will prove my point: love does kill in the end, or causes a lot of pain, at least." And he handed Reuben a sheet of paper with Reuben's proposed statement already typed on it.

Reuben read it. It looked okay. The Devil had agreed to his terms.

Reuben made a left at the corner by the fried chicken joint, stopped. There she was, his lady. Radiant as ever. He began to tremble; he couldn't believe it was actually happening. God, my baby. Marcy was dressed in a snug-fitting white blouse, designer jeans, heels. She looked better than any woman he'd ever seen. She ran to him, and they embraced.

"Honey, is it really you?" Reuben said, stopping to take a good look.

His lady smiled, kissed him on the lips, looked into his eyes again. They were just about at the same height level with those high heels she wore. "It's good to see you, Reuben."

She noticed the car. Reuben explained he had borrowed it from a friend.

"Not the same one I talked to?" And she began to describe the Devil; said he'd been driving a car just like the Mustang Reuben had pulled up in.

"Same one," Reuben said. He would save the surprise for later; let her know that the car was to be hers.

"He finally helped me see the light," Marcy said. They got in the car, and Reuben got the idea to drive out to the ocean, north of Malibu and stay at a motel out there, away from Hollywood and its garbage. And they stayed up all night talking about everything that had happened to them during those past eighteen months. A couple of times they both wept and held each other and finally dozed off as the sun came up.

Marcy was still sound asleep when the Devil tapped Reuben on the shoulder around noon. The Devil held the contract in his hand, and he gave Reuben the fountain pen to sign his name with. Reuben hesitated.

"What now?" the Devil said. Reuben slid out of bed, and they stepped outside to talk on the balcony.

"You're playing games with me, Reuben."

"Look, your whole idea is insane. I don't want to walk along some ledge. It's crazy. Besides, I haven't got the guts—"

"You said you'd do it; you were ready to on your own, remember?"

"Yes, I know—but—why do you think I stayed in that room for so long? Only because I didn't have the guts to take a dive, no balls. I was trying to do it with the booze. It seemed an easier out. Please don't ask me to do something that screwy."

"You scratch my nuts, I'll scratch yours. Remember, Reuben?"

"Please, can't you think of something else? A little less risky? What would she think if she ever found out? I mean, the loony, idiotic things I did before—well, I think she understands why I acted like that back then . . . but for me to do something like that *now* . . . She'd think I was loony."

The Devil shrugged. "Suit yourself, Reuben."

"Can we please discuss it later? I just want to spend every moment with her. I'd like to buy her breakfast. Surprise her, you know? With breakfast in bed. I want us to get married; I just want to be a good husband to this lady. We'll talk, okay?" Reuben went inside, closing the balcony door behind him.

Marcy was awake, sitting up in bed. And she wasn't smiling.

"I feel like shit," she said. "And you look like shit."

She got up, got into her clothes and heels, and walked in the bathroom. She shut the door. A moment later Reuben heard the toilet flush. The door opened and Marcy was standing in front of the full-length mirror that hung from it, brushing her long hair.

"I don't know what made me come back," she said. "You're a loser, Reuben. Always will be. I guess I just wanted to prove to myself once and for all that we never had it, never did."

"We did," Reuben insisted.

"Nope. Never did. It was infatuation; it was sex. I don't love you. We can stay friends if you like, although I can't see the point."

"Marcy, what are you saying?"

She was back in the john. Held the toothbrush under the tap and brushed her teeth that way without applying toothpaste. Reached for her lipstick. Applied a light coat to lower and upper lip.

"Honey, you can't mean that."

"Come on, Reuben. Let's be realistic, all right? I mean, look at you—*would you just look at you.* Do you realize what I left in Vegas? Do you have any idea?"

"You said he was a creep."

She shrugged. "Did I? He's a great lay, though, and he knows how to have a good time."

Reuben sat on the edge of the bed. "I thought you came back because you needed me. . . . What a fool. . . ." His eyes had tears in them.

Marcy stood sideways in front of the medicine cabinet mirror, took a deep breath, holding her stomach in, and studied as her breasts rose. Satisfied, she walked out of the bathroom, paused at the front door.

"Don't feel bad, Reuben. It was never meant to be, that's all." And she left.

The tears flowed like a river now. The pain was back; it had returned, that churning knot of pain in his guts, the cramps he had almost learned how to deal with, now it was back, much worse—and it was all that cocksucker's fault, the fucking Devil's fault.

Reuben shot up out of bed and out to the balcony.

"Where the hell are you, you evil son of a bitch!"

There was no one out there, not the Devil, not his Marcy, not anyone, just a parking lot with some cars and the ocean. Reuben spotted his answer down the street: a liquor store. When he returned to finish dressing, the Devil was hanging from a corner of the ceiling, a hairy ape with a slick red ass. He walked on all fours across the ceiling laughing in mockery; laughing, laughing.

"You did that, didn't you?"

The Devil farted. That was his answer. Motherfucker.

"Didn't you? You made her change like that. If that's the way it's going to be I don't want any part of it. I don't want her like that—no, it's no good. Sure, you can *make her* want me—only I don't want her that way. I couldn't."

"You'll take her any way you can get her."

"No!"

"Come on, Reuben."

"No, man! I couldn't. I want her to love me. I'd want her to be with me because she wants to and for no other reason!"

"Relax, Reuben. You don't have to shout. I'm right here, right here, baby."

Reuben sat on the edge of the bed and remained quiet. The Devil continued to laugh. Reuben got up, took a leak in the john, slapped cold water on his face. He walked to the liquor store, bought a bottle of bourbon, returned to the room. He stretched out on the bed, the bottle cradled in his arms.

He closed his eyes, didn't move. The tears had stopped, the pain was no longer there. A numbness had overtaken his body. Even his brain was numb. There were no images there, nothing, no words. It was dark. He was inside that tunnel, and there was no sign of light. None.

He opened his eyes. Reached over for one of the tumblers on the end table. Poured a double into it. Set it down on the dresser. Got a second tumbler. Poured the same amount. Recapped the bottle. Left it in his lap. Held the tumbler out to the Devil. He reached for the one on the dresser for himself.

"Drink?"

The ape dropped from the ceiling, landed on his hind legs, and walked like that over to the bed. Took the tumbler. They looked at each other.

"Let's drink to chaos," the Devil said.

Reuben shrugged. "Why not?"

They drank them down. Reuben poured more bourbon into the glasses, and said: "I'd like to propose a toast to the *Devil*."

"Oh?"

"Because you can get by without giving a fuck. You do without. Anybody like that deserves a toast."

"To the Devil," the Devil said. Down went half the contents in each tumbler. Reuben studied him now, and he had to smile. He was drinking with a monkey, a fucking monkey, but it was all right, he had finally met him, finally, the one guy nobody ever saw, the main *heavy*, the one so many were scared shitless of, he was drinking with now, yes.

"To lust," Reuben proposed. "To bigotry, to racism, to infidelity, to crime, to rape, to killing, to bloodshed, to hatred and vengeance, to suicide jockeys."

The baboon was laughing and scratching his ass. They drank them up. A third round was poured.

"You come up with something," Reuben suggested.

The monkey nodded. "I most certainly will: to back-stabbing, to knifings, to heart attacks, to robberies, maiming, hangings, to divorce, breakups and breakdowns—"

"Right on!" Reuben applauded. "To breakups!"

"To VD, herpes, malaria, to puss, to zits, to small pox, rheumatism, bleeding ulcers, to heartbreak, to pain and all the rest! Ha ha!"

They drank up.

Reuben cleared his throat. "Can I ask you something?"

The monkey nodded.

"If you were able to manipulate her like that—why the thing about the ledge? Hell, you could have gotten me to do that just like that." And Reuben snapped his fingers.

"Right," the Devil said. "I'll tell you: because you're still going to do it, only you'll do it a lot sooner."

"You think so?"

The monkey nodded. "Yep."

"Know something? I never thought I'd like you. Know what I mean? You're okay. Yessir; all right."

"Yes, Reuben, you're going to take that dive after all."

"I guess so," Reuben said under his breath. "I guess you're right. You still want the suicide note?"

"Why not? The icing on the cake, don't you think?"

"Exactly."

A piece of paper and a fountain pen materialized in the ape's free paw. Reuben took it, started writing. He made it brief, to the point. "You mind if I don't lay too much shit on her, you know? The blame? Hell, we could just say I was tired of living, and it had nothing to do with a woman."

The monkey made a face, like he really didn't care for it, like he wasn't sure.

"Why not?" Reuben wanted to know.

The monkey nodded. "Shit, go ahead."

"Thanks."

Reuben finished scribbling the note, signed it. Let the monkey see it.

"Good," the monkey said. They drove to Reuben's fleabag in town, and continued drinking into the night until they both passed out. Reuben was set on taking that dive first thing the next morning. The Devil liked that.

My Kind of Client
A Choo-Choo Buschitski Private Eye Episode

"Bullshit!"

That was what she said and kept on saying. *"Bullshit, Choo-Choo!"*

"All right, Rita—settle down," I told her, but she wouldn't hear of it. We were in my office. She held the hem of her form-fitting black dress up and continued to pace the floor in her crotchless panties and heels while I sat behind the desk in my swivel trying to pull on a bottle of cold Coors. She was furious, and maybe it was understandable. I'd tracked down Manny, her runaway common-law husband and told her, according to my rules, I don't ball married and/or attached women. We'd fucked during the whole time I was looking for Manny, but now that he was found I wanted to stop seeing her.

"But I don't love him, Choo-Choo," she pleaded. "Can't you see what I'm trying to tell you here? Sure, he's hung, but so what? He's stupid and he's dull! I can't stand being around the scum bucket! I can't stand it."

"He needs you, Rita," I said, not that I knew what I was talking about. Mostly I was just plain tired of banging the same pee hole. I wanted something different, new. Besides, this Manny was the jealous type, and he was partial to shanks. He'd left half a dozen men with foot long scars to remember him by—and I don't think any of them had actually shagged his precious Rita.

"He doesn't care about me. It's all some macho bullshit to prove that he runs my life. *Goddamn it, he's a creep!* We're not married, not even engaged to be married!"

"I've got a client due in fifteen minutes."

"To hell with your fucking client," she screamed. "I'm talking about you and me, Choo-Choo. You and me. Didn't I treat you right? Didn't I?"

I pulled on my bottle. "Maybe later on—if he splits again," I said. It was nice being on the other end. I'd been in her position too damn many times. "I don't want to hurt you, precious, but it's just not being practical. This Manny of yours is a lunatic. I don't want to end up with a butcher knife sticking out of my back. I can take care of myself, sure—still—"

"Oh, fuck you!"

She dropped the hem of her dress, grabbed her purse and slammed the door on her way out.

I emptied the bottle and got another. I sighed. What the hell, that's life. Can't please everyone. Just can't be done. Why get worked up about things we have no control over?

This next dame that was due any minute hadn't sounded all that great over the phone, like maybe she had a permanent sore throat or something, and I expected an older woman, but when she walked in I got an instant woody. There was nothing old about her. She was tall, hair that was dark and long and had a shine like velvet.

She sat down, fished around in her purse and pulled out a foot-long vibrator, asked to please not mind her, hiked up her dress and jammed that thing up her cunt.

What the hell? This was a first. A woman masturbating right in front of me and we hadn't even been properly introduced. After a while, she moaned a couple of times and slumped limply against the back rest of her chair. I'm slow at times; finally I made it over to where she sat, was down on my knees with my tongue hanging out when she sat up, drawing a .32 from her purse.

"What do you think you're doing, schmuck?"

"Just wanted to see if you were still breathing," I said, returning to my desk and my beer.

"I don't fuck men," she said, still aiming that gun at me. "All I do is masturbate."

"It's a free country," I told her.

"No hassles that way. No pain, no bullshit."

"In other words you're not looking for a relationship. That what you're saying?"

She stowed the piece, and fired up a smoke. She inhaled and subsequently exhaled like a star from the silver screen. She lowered the hem of her skirt and stood up.

"You any good?" she asked.

"That's what I wanted to show you."

She chuckled. "You know what I mean."

I guess I did.

"Depends what you want done." Then I did *my* number: pulled my meat out, got a girly mag open to the centerfold, spread it across the desk and started stroking.

"What kind of shit is this?" she demanded.

"If you think I'm gonna let you give me blue balls, you're nuts."

She chuckled some more. "I get it," she said. "Go right ahead."

I did. I even got a small bottle of lube out, applied a few drops to my right palm and ran it over the head of my cock. Goddamn, it felt great. The dame was smiling. Then I thought of something. "Would you do me a small favor—" I said.

"I don't fuck men I don't know."

"Oh no, nothing like that."

"What then?"

"Would you just kind of lift your skirt up?" She did. "Bend over and turn around." She did. That well-rounded ass sticking out at me, and that hairy beaver directly underneath did it; I was about to explode and knew it would be a lot of fucking Twinkie filling all over the fucking place. It was then the dame did something I hadn't expected at all. She was on her knees, in front of me with her mouth open. She had her tongue going up and down the length of my pole. She stroked it with her hand and took it inside her mouth, just about all of it. I jammed it farther in and shot juice down her throat and screamed as I did.

"Oh goddamn," I sighed.

She licked it clean and stood up. I offered her the beer and watched her take a healthy pull. Then I did the same. We were both grinning now.

"Thanks," I said. "You're great."

"You ain't seen nothing yet, Jack," she countered.

"So you need a private eye," I said to her.

"Maybe."

"Meaning what?"

"Meaning if you're not good enough—you could get killed."

"Explain."

"I was robbed by my ex. He got $50,000 worth in jewels."

"No sweat," I said.

"He's connected," she said. "Runs with a tough bunch. They kill people and stuff," she said. "You still up to it?"

"What's in it for me?"

"Your fee, of course," she said. "And maybe a bonus."

"I want to fuck you for about three weeks," I said. "As long as I bring the jewels in, of course."

"You got it."

"I'd want you to literally be my slave for that period of time."

"You got it. I'll do anything you ask—but first, you've got to come back alive."

I got a black-and-white photo from her, the full name: Randy "Ratso" Ratner. The face in the photo had a pug nose, unibrow and a pockmarked complexion. His lips were thick and his upper choppers were missing. The hair was cut so short that it made him appear practically bald. Large ears and nose. She named a couple of bars where he usually hung out, a motel in East Hollywood.

"Any other info?"

"I'm serious about the crowd he runs with."

I finished off the bottle, pulled the bottom drawer out and stuck a small piece into the holster strapped to my calf. I slid the .38 into my shoulder rig. Then I checked to see if the stiletto was intact inside my right sleeve. Good. I was all set, except for one little detail.

"All set," I told her. "Except for one little detail: I need a retainer of two hundred bucks."

"After I just gave you the best head of your entire fucking life?"

I nodded. "And I'm serious about that three weeks. I'm gonna want it."

"That's okay, but two hundred up front?"

"I got overhead. Bullets don't grow on trees."

She produced a checkbook.

I smiled.

"No checks."

She looked at me, then came up with the cash. I didn't say anything.

"You got a nice-looking cock," she said, and was gone. I wouldn't say I'm impossible to deal with; I don't like being a pushover.

I had a case, some cash, and three weeks of righteous shagging to look forward to. And she had the kind of legs and butt that made my mouth water. Great. Truly fucking great. I programmed the machine to pick up any incoming messages, grabbed my fedora and stepped outside.

The pathetic-looking dames working the massage parlor downstairs were giving me their spiel again in a second.

"We know why you don't ever come in," they said. "Ya think we gots the clap. Shit, we clean, man. We clean, Choo-Choo."

"Yeah," I chuckled. "And Capone didn't die of syphilis, either."

"Faggot cocksucker!" they screamed in tandem. A wino hit me up for a buck before I'd reached my burnt auburn Caddy Fleetwood. But that was something I never minded, giving the rummies a buck or two. What the hell, I understood. They kept the punks from molesting my wheels. And no, the Caddy is not new. Far from it. But it looks nice enough to impress certain clients. People who knew me knew I was barely making ends meet. Hey, sometimes show is all you've got. I probably should have relocated out of the neighborhood a long time ago. It wasn't skid row exactly, although it came pretty damn close.

I turned the key in the ignition and made it up Alvarado to Sunset. I hung a left on Sunset and took it west. It started to rain. By the time I reached the first bar on my list it was pouring down. Not cats and dogs exactly, maybe only cats and cats. I was lucky and found a parking space but two doors away and ran inside the joint. It smelled like the zoo: stale shit and urine. It was a wino convention in there. Drunks in stained and worn clothing. They had a pinball machine in there, a video machine, pool table. Two dykes with butch haircuts were working the pool table. I recognized them. They were okay. These two didn't hate men. The chunky barkeep with the infected red nose was Dudley "Birdbrain." His real surname was Birdsong. Yes, he had shit for brains. That's exactly how he ended up with that handle. But he wasn't a bad sort. He'd given me a beer now and then when I was down and needed one. He was cool.

I moseyed up to the bar, ordered a whiskey with beer chaser and showed Dudley the photo. Dudley stared for a moment and proceeded to wipe the sweat from the mess of warts on his forehead.

"Boy, Choo-Choo," was all he said. "Oh boy."

"S'matter?"

"Oh boy."

"You seen him or not?"

"Yeah, sure."

"Yeah, sure what?"

"He's been in here." The sweat poured. He kept wiping.

"Spit it out, man. What day? What time? Who with?"

"He was here the other night, Choo-Choo. Stuck around 'till about closing time. He wasn't alone. Rough customer, that one," he added.

"So I've heard." I ordered another whiskey with beer chaser, lit a Pall Mall.

"The goons that was with him looked like killers. Scarred mugs. They was packin' roscoes, Choo-Choo. An' the scars; shoulda seen the scars on their mugs."

I looked at him.

"Ugliest lookin' scars I ever seen. One had part of his ear missin'. An' that ain't all. This Ratso Ratner—his lower lip was blue, like he'd just been in a bad scrape, if you know what I mean."

Dudley's breath was starting to get to me. I blew smoke in his face and that kind of made him back off a bit.

"You expect they'll be back?"

"Sure, why not? That video game over there?" He indicated that video game over there. "The owner just bought it from them about a week ago. That's what this guy Ratner does, I guess. Sells video games, pinball machines, shit like that."

"You been a real sweetheart, Dudley," I told him. "I'd kiss you if ya wasn't so damn ugly."

"Just do me a favor, Felix," Dudley Birdbrain said. "I like you. Don't get yourself blown away."

I left the bar with intentions of coming back later. I needed to go out and find a backup man, or maybe the bozo I'd used before. That's how I've managed to survive this long in this racket. A good backup man adds years to your life expectancy. I needed a motherfucker who knew how to use a shotgun.

I got in the old Caddy. If it was coming down like cats and cats earlier, it sure as hell had progressed to cats and dogs presently. I headed further west on Sunset, hung a right at Normandie, took it a block north of Hollywood Boulevard and I was there, a run-down, two-story, gray stucco, thirty-year-old building that should have been condemned the moment construction ended on it. Instead it was christened the *Happy Arms Complex.* There were a lot of buildings like this in this part of LA with cute names that didn't fit. Homely and Depressing, (not to mention decrepit), would have been a more appropriate moniker for the eyesore.

The backup man I'd used before had a leg missing, lost it in the 'Nam war, and don't ask me why they called him One-Eyed Joe, because there was nothing the matter with Joe "Scumbucket" Slowinski's coal dark eyes. And for a guy with a missing leg he got around pretty good with the artificial one; and he'd do anything for a pill, any kind of pill, any time. He was the manager of the Happy Arms Complex. Only ones happy must have been the rodents.

I knocked on the manager's door.

"It's open!" a male voice shouted from inside. I opened the door just a crack at first, then shoved it farther in with my foot. Nothing, no sound.

"It's me, One-Eye," I announced.

"Come on in, Buschitski."

I walked in, slowly.

One-Eye was watching *Casablanca* on a black-and-white portable with the sound off from his recliner and he had his shotgun cradled in his arms. Hell, I shook my head and had to grin. Him and his goddamn shotgun, always in his lap and/or within easy reach. He turned the sound up on the movie.

"Good ol' One-Eyed Joe."

"How goes it, Buschitski?"

"Got a job for you."

He reached for his OD green fatigue jacket. Stood up. "Let's go."

"Hold your horses, One-Eye. Hold on."

He lowered himself back into his raggedy chair. Come to think of it, the whole place looked raggedy. An army of ants worked their way toward the kitchen floor.

I explained the setup to him and laid a fifty on him. One-Eye smiled. He liked that. He liked it even more after I told him about Ratso Ratner and his goons.

"When do we go?"

"Later tonight," I told him. "I'll let you know." Not being able to take the stink any longer, not to mention being assaulted by ants, I egressed.

I found a chop suey joint not far from KTTV and dialed my office number. I have one of these gadgets that allows me to play back my messages. The first message was from Rita.

"*I'm gonna kill you, you bastard!*" the voice screamed. "*You just don't fuckin' care! I'm gonna kill youoooo!*" I sighed. Dizzy dame. My second and only other message was from a potential client who wanted his "harlot of a wife" tracked down. I returned to my table where my hot tea and chop suey awaited me.

I ate my chop suey and couldn't stop thinking about the brunette who had sucked me off so well in my office. My cock was stirring and I thought about pulling on it right there and then in the Chinese joint. Then it dawned on me. I hadn't remembered to even ask her name. It wasn't all that important. For my files maybe. One had to pay some attention at least when it came to names of clients and billing. The professional way to be.

The second call I placed to Dudley Birdbrain.

"They're here all right, Choo-Choo," he said. "They sure are."

"Thanks, Dudley."

I drove by One-Eyed Joe's, picked him up, and we were on our way. I guided the Caddy down the alley in back of the bar and stopped at the rear exit. One-Eye got out. Only thing was the door was locked and would have to be opened from inside.

"Looks like it'll have to be opened from inside," One-Eye said.

"No shit, One-Eye," I said, and pulled away. I double-parked it in front of the bar, flashers flashing. This wasn't going to take long. I went in. Ratso Ratner and his goons were at a table all by themselves playing cards.

I walked in the back, let One-Eye in. My instructions to One-Eye were to wait for my signal, which was to be a simple: YO. Then I returned to the front.

I walked up to the table where the dirtbags sat playing poker and said to Ratso Ratner: "Telephone call for you."

The dirtbag looked up at me. "For me?"

"No, for your mother."

"Wiseass," he said under his breath, then came up with a backhand that sent me reeling against the pool table. I got an assist from Myrna, one of the dykes. I winked at her and told her I was okay. I think she understood I was working. I had the stiletto pressed against Ratso Ratner's ribs as he reached for the phone behind the bar.

"What's going on?" he said.

"We're taking a ride."

"Bullshit," he said.

I pressed the blade further in to make sure he got the point. He nodded. "Whatever you say, boss."

One of his goons finally realized something wasn't quite kosher and went for his shoulder rig. My stiletto hissed through the smoke-filled air and stopped in the scumbag's throat. Ratso Ratner made a move. I sent a solid fist up into his nuts that quickly made him change his mind as he went down. The third goon got a hard whack across the face with a cue stick from Myrna.

Everything was under control, and there hadn't even been any need for One-Eye's assistance. He would probably be pissed about that. But what the hell. One-eye came in anyway with a displeased look on his face. He'd been itching to use the shotgun and the opportunity had been blown for him.

I winked at him.

"Hell," sighed One-Eye.

I relieved Ratso Ratner of his piece and shoved him outside toward the Caddy.

"Where we goin'?" he wanted to know.

"I was hired to retrieve the stolen jewels," I explained, and started up the car. A loud blast ensued from inside the bar. I cuffed Ratner to the car door and hurried inside. The third goon's body was splayed across the top of the green velvet of the pool table, his chest having been busted wide open. One-Eye was standing at the other end of the room, the shotgun smoking. Blood flowed from Myrna's left leg.

"The bastard tried to kill me," Myrna said, indicating the dead hood. "One-Eye over there saved me."

I returned to the Caddy, un-cuffed and shoved Ratso inside and we pulled away.

"Where to?" I said.

"Them jewels don't belong to Trixie," Ratner said. "They's mine. I give 'em to her when we was together. The stuff's mine, I tell ya."

"Oh yeah? She says different."

"This is all wrong," he said. "So I give ya the rocks—so what?"

"I give 'em back to her."

"An' I go back and get 'em again."

"Not if I kill you."

"Why would you do that?"

"I like to do a job right when I'm hired."

"Maybe you ain't figured it out yet: I'm connected."

"I think it's all a rumor. Who'd want to be connected to dog shit like you?"

"Hey, man, you want the jewels? Okay. There ain't no need for disrespec'. Ain't no need for name callin'. I ain't dog shit—never was dog shit. I'm jus' doin' a job—tryin' ta get a business started. Hell, that's why that bitch is pissed: I wouldn't give her a piece of the action—"

I farted. Ratso Ratner rolled his window down.

"I been sellin' lots of these pinball machines, video games, porno movies. Shit sells like hot cakes."

"I'm still waiting for an address, Ratner."

"Go to Yucca," he said. "And turn up Ivar." I did. A depressing neighborhood, especially in this kind of gloomy weather. All kinds of garbage floated down into the sewers from the top of the hill. The Caddy huffed and puffed up Ivar—like I said, it's not a new car—until we reached a bleak-looking wood frame with its lights out. The wire fence in front barely withstood the wind.

We got out. Ratner was my shield as we proceeded toward the front door. When we reached the porch, the door blew open and I pulled Ratner down with me. Nothing else happened.

"It's the fucking wind," Ratner said. "Just the wind."

I guess it was. We went in. Ratner flipped a light switch. What was the living room was filled with stereos, color TV sets, vacuum cleaners, Tiffany lamps, boxes and boxes of porno cassettes, vinyl record albums. Over in one of the corners a rat about a foot and a half long scampered over a carton of Sony head stereos. Shit, I'd been meaning to get one of those for weeks (head set, not a rat).

I checked out the other rooms with Ratner. The room in the back was much bigger and housed about twenty pinball machines, boxes of dildos and marital aids, a pile of black umbrellas and a stack of slick publications on anal sex.

Ratner took me down in the basement that was full of more similar items. Goddamn, what didn't this low-life cocksucker deal in? He pushed a battered old dresser to the side and opened the wall safe behind it. The jewels were in a leather pouch. He handed them over. I couldn't tell if the stuff was genuine, but what the hell. It looked okay. I would have a jeweler check it over later, or maybe I would just pull back the hammer on my .38 and jam the business end into Ratner's schnoz and have him tell me the truth.

We went back upstairs and Ratner fixed us some hot coffee while I poured through the ass fucking magazines. The stuff was making me hard. They had pictures of women sucking huge cocks and licking assholes, pictures of men with large pricks banging tight female butts. The shit was making me horny. I couldn't take it. I kept thinking of my client and what I was going to do to her as soon as I saw her again. I took a sip of the coffee and had to spit it out. You expected as much.

"The fuck you got in here, Ratner? Ink?"

He shrugged and continued drinking from his mug. I walked over to the carton of Sony Walkman stereos. There was another rat behind it, or maybe it was the same one. I aimed and squeezed off a shot and watched the motherfucker splatter against the wall.

"You don't give a shit about much, do you?" Ratner said.

I ripped open a carton, picked out a Walkman. Shoved a battery in. Then I found several cassettes of Beethoven's music. I inserted his Fifth. Got the earphones on. I couldn't believe the sound that came through. *Incredible! Just fucking incredible!* I stuffed two of the porn magazines in my trench coat, the stereo and cassettes, and paused at the door. . . .

"If the stuff turns out to be imitation," I told Ratner, and I was talking about the gems, "I'll be back . . . and I'll kill you."

"I believe you would," Ratner said, then he shrugged. "What I get for fucking around with a cunt."

I drove to my room near Sixth and Union and called the brunette to give her the news. Trixie was ecstatic to hear it. Then I told her where I lived and what to bring with her, exactly the kind of lingerie I liked to see her in, to bring enough food to last us at least a week, enough booze, and to make it snappy, then I plopped down on my bed and started going through the magazines again.

The tip of my cock was wet. Pre-cum. I was ready.

The dame showed up with everything I'd wanted: black heels, black fishnets, garter belt, crotchless panties, black negligees, etc. Then I had her get in the tub with me and we rubbed soap suds over each other's bodies. She kept asking about the jewels. I showed them to her, and returned them to my wall safe.

"You got to fuck me dry, bitch—and the stuff is all yours."

She smiled. "Like I said, honey, I like your prick."

"I like your cunt, baby, your beautiful asshole, your long legs, your tits. I want to suck your tits, your nipples. I want to lick you all over, every inch of you. . . ."

I lubed her asshole, slid my middle finger deep up it.

"Does that hurt?" I asked.

She only smiled and did the same to me. I liked it. I withdrew my finger and got my pulsing chubby in there and stroked. Goddamn, it was wonderful. I gave her about twenty or thirty strokes and unloaded and clung to her with all my might.

After we rinsed the soap off, we made it over to the bed. I smoked a cigarette and listened to Beethoven while she fixed us steaks and mojo potatoes, a salad. We would both need our strength for the next three weeks.

When dinner was ready I sat at the table and was soon hard again. I snapped my fingers and she was down there under the table, lapping it up. I raised my legs and her tongue found my butt. She drove it on in there as I instructed.

"Deeper, bitch," I said to her. "Don't be shy. Get it deeper, deeper."

After a while my legs got tired and I had to lower them. She worked away on my hairy nuts, taking them in her mouth: first one at a time, then both at the same time, then she worked on my cock while I worked away on the tasty steak. I felt the cum brewing in my loins and got the Walkman on, turned up the volume, sat back and watched. Those pretty lips sucked and sucked, the tongue working away relentlessly. She stroked it, pausing only briefly to add more saliva to the shaft and continued. The music played in my ears. At about the time I was ready to shoot cream, I pulled it out, lifted her clean off the floor and dropped her on the bed and drove it inside her wet cunt. It took four strokes and I filled her with juice. Both of us plopped down against the bed afterwards. Some rest was due in order. There was lots of fornicating to look forward to in the coming weeks.

Bone

A PI Choo-Choo Buschitski Long Short

I don't rile easy—and when I do get pissed it hardly ever lasts. I don't hold a grudge (with a few exceptions; there are always exceptions). I see blood red over a dog being kicked or a kid being slapped around. I hate to see anybody go hungry. I'll give money to bums whenever I got any to give. And, oh yeah, there's nothing better I like to do than shag (or eat) pussy. That's not to say I can get it up for just anything in a dress. I got my type. Thin ones leave me limp, and when they're too heavy, that doesn't do it, either. I like them large-boned, with long healthy legs and wide hips. I like them in heels and black stockings and garter belt. I like a woman to have an athletic, large ass and heavy tits with nipples prominent enough to suck on. I like it when they laugh loud and often and especially when they go down on me—and between all that, I like to be alone. It's my nature. I'm a private dick for a living. I'll sleep late, drink beer and do as I please; (usually) I don't like to put things back where they belong. I'm not the tidiest person in the world. It drives some bitches crazy (I don't like that type hanging around very long). I bathe when I feel like it (which is rarely). I'm a motherfucking winner. The name—remember this— is Felix "Choo-Choo" Buschitski. I'm good at what I do. I've kicked ass in my time and had my ass kicked as well. I've been kind and I've been mean and stark raving mad. I've had my share of hangovers and shed more than a river over a female or two. Yeah, I've shed some tears—but don't you fucking make the mistake and take me for a pushover—and don't start in about the ERA or Male (Confusion) Liberation. That kind of shit just makes me want to fart (in response). Men are men and women are women—and we can all be such babies at times—and at other times we act right and grown-up. We all have our bad days—and we have some luck now and then. I can't stand being around mopers, misery mongers, complainers, bigots, loud-mouth braggarts and the like. And once I do a job for you—don't come back. I don't ever want to see your ass again. Once a job is done—it's over. I forget you ever existed (unless you owe me money). It may sound cold (and maybe it is), so be it. I don't like going over the same bullshit twice.

Now that we got that out of the way, now that we know each other— you know more about me than I do about you (true, right?).

Let me tell you what happened. This one is titled: **BONE.** Could be the title has something to do with the fact that I'm constantly walking around with a woody. Thirty years old, always thinking about pussy, tang; either thinking about it, licking it, or banging it. I was born over-sexed. If it sounds like brag, *it ain't*; on the contrary, it can be a burden. Try beating your meat ten times a day for fourteen years. Shit, half the time I can't get up out of bed. Just plain too tired, always tired. The times I do manage to get out there and on a case, it is a relief— because, man, the body and the nuts need a chance to recharge. You have to let the balls recharge.

The last big cry I'd had over losing a woman had been about four years back—and since then, I've got myself trained to accept it as an inevitable fact of life. They always go. There is something that inevitably tells them they must move on. Like I said, the last big cry was four years ago—and since then it takes me a week, five days, seven at the most. If she's gone, so is the memory of her. And you know something? It's a rather pleasant way of dealing with things. Seven days. Then I go out, do something, take on a case, find another babe, etc.

That's what I was doing Friday night on November 3rd—I was sitting in Winchell's in West Hollywood and toughing out days number six and seven.

She had been good, the type I go for—and she had been the veteran of many wars (the male/female type), many many affairs. That heart had been well protected. I didn't hear from her—and she didn't hear from me. We both knew where we lived. We both hadn't bothered to change our phone number. The warriors battled on. I hadn't slept in two days, hadn't shaved or bathed. I was sipping a cup of decaffeinated joe and eating a chocolate-covered doughnut and watching the sleaze outside.

It was 10:30 at night. I'd been waiting for the client for a good half hour. A man. I didn't know much about him, other than that he'd be wearing a purple suit. He said his name was Black. Maybe he was black too. He sounded like he might be from New York.

Someone entered Winchell's. I looked in the direction of the door. The guy was in a purple suit. Mr. Black.

"You Choo-Choo Buschitski?" he asked.

I rose to my feet. We shook hands.

"Man," he said, "you look like you spent some time in hell, brother."

"Getting over a death in the family," I said.

"Sorry to hear it, brother," he said.

I offered to buy him coffee and a doughnut. "No, thanks, man," he declined politely. "Can't handle that stuff."

Then we got down to the nitty-gritty. The guy wanted me to find his sister. They had just come out from the East Coast, about a month ago, and she'd been missing for four days. I asked for a photo. He produced one. The girl was pretty and there was a slight resemblance. I told him I needed a hundred bucks up front. He didn't have it, not all of it. Forty bucks was all he had. After contemplating for a moment, I took it. I needed to stay busy. He mentioned that he had decided to return to New York at the end of the month, and hoped to find his sister by then.

"LA just don't agree with me, man. Just ain't right for me."

I smiled. Hell, I had always hated the cocksucking town. But why I stayed on I had never been able to answer.

He gave me a card with his name and phone number where he could be reached, and was gone. I looked at the card: Lloyd Black. I wondered what the guy did for a living.

Forty bucks.

One couldn't do much with forty bucks. Not the way I liked to operate. I feed the whores and the gigolos along the Strip and Santa Monica Boulevard. I also liked to feed some of the bartenders in *both* the *gay and straight* joints. One got info (if indeed there was any info to be had) reasonably fast that way.

I walked to Crescent Heights and stood on the corner. A young hustler in a white wifebeater and dirty tight jeans gave me a nasty look, like I was taking over his territory or something. I showed him the photo Lloyd Black had given me just for the hell of it.

The idiot had an idiotic look on his face.

"I don't go for chicks, man," he said in what sounded like a whisper with a lisp.

"Ya seen her anywhere, man? Her brother's worried sick she may be in trouble."

"You a cop?"

You pathetic cocksucker, I felt like saying. I hate that fucking line: *ARE YOU A COP?* I don't make the goddamn jack they do—and my dick only gets to probe the stuff that they aren't able to get to (too often).

I shook my head. "No, nothing like that."

He gave me the once-over, dumber than ever.

"Ever watch Canon, man?—or Barnaby Jones or—"

"No," he said. "I never watch that shit on TV—"

"I don't either, bro. I'm a private dick."

"Hey, I ain't never seen that ho," and he turned away, stuck the thumb out. I walked east on the boulevard, reluctantly went in the first gay joint on the block.

Rufus had a thick stash, a flattop. He looked like a macho drill sergeant, only he was a pussycat. He was making good tips. The bar was hopping. I waved a fin his way; showed him the still.

"Not many females come in here," he said, "as you well know, Choo-Choo, not ones with a twat, anyway."

I looked about the place. There were maybe four women out of some thirty customers. "Sure, now and then, usually out-of-towners who don't know better, or else dykes."

He was right. I had him look at it again. He didn't give me a no right away. "Could have been her. . . . I can't say." He looked up at me. "I'm not racist, man. . . . Hell, we got enough shit to contend with. Some of these black chicks . . . I couldn't tell them apart. Like the old joke: they all look alike. But it's the fucking truth. She could have been in here."

"Okay; you're not sure. Was she alone?"

"The babe I saw, the one I think was here—no, she was not alone. She was with another white chick and a tall white dude, possibly straight, blond or reddish-blond hair. I couldn't say."

I thanked Rufus, asked him to keep an eye out, and left.

Progress. She was in the neighborhood. *Possibly.*

The next bar was half and half—half gay/half straight. What I can't stand about men is when they start in about their conquests—like the one with the ugly red nose who walked up to me out of nowhere. "I ripped that bitch apart," he said. "Got her in the asshole, but good. She couldn't stand up afterwards, couldn't walk. Ripped her good."

"You did shit," I said, making it to the bar. "Probably got three inches and cream in two strokes." It was obvious he'd had a few drinks in him because when he made his move to swing it looked pathetic and clumsy, his fist barely clipping my chin. He didn't have much height on me, but he was husky. I wanted to knock that red nose off for him and sent four hard knuckles directly into it. He started to go down and one of the waiters caught him just in time, breaking red nose's fall. Some of the red nose's blood got on the waiter. I was asked to leave.

How do you like that? 86'd because I didn't like some shitbag's alcoholic nose. He did take the first swing, didn't he?

There's a small parklike area near the Starwood. I walked over to the bus bench where one of these bag ladies sat, her Hushpuppy and shopping cart (full of literally junk) nearby. I'd seen her before, plenty of times, and had always wanted to ask her about the dog. There was something awful familiar about that damn dog. I don't know if you can recall the Hushpuppy commercials, but her hound looked just like the one they used years ago. That was what I asked her. She smiled and shook her head. "People always ask me that," she said. She wondered if

I might have a cigarette. I didn't, but gave her some money instead. She thanked me. I found out stuff about her. She was forty-eight, had a mother still alive and living near Pico and Robertson. Her mother did a lot of socializing, had lots of friends over, but she rarely went to see her. She preferred living the way she did. I didn't exactly buy it, didn't feel like belaboring the point, either. I showed her the photo. Yeah, she'd seen the girl—and she gave me basically the same info Rufus had given me: with another white girl and a tall blond guy.

"How long ago was this?"

"Oh . . . two days ago."

"Can you recall which direction they were headed in?"

"That way."

She pointed west, down Santa Monica Boulevard.

"Up Holloway," she said. "Saw them by the 7-Eleven, then they went up Holloway."

"How did she look? Happy? Sad?"

She shrugged.

I thanked her, and walked to the Caddy. I pulled into the 7-Eleven at the corner of Holloway and LaCienega and talked to the kid behind the counter with the scabs and zits on his face. He was gay. I think maybe he was interested in me. I went through the routine again. He kept nodding. "Yes, I remember. Fanny—that's what they called her."

"How about the tall guy? Remember his name? Or maybe the other girl's name?"

"Either Skip or Scott, something like that. The white chick's name was Carol—at least that's what the black chick, Fanny, kept calling her."

I would have slid a fiver his way, except I didn't have any to give.

Sitting in the Caddy, I didn't know what the hell else to do other than to start driving up and down the Strip, and that's what I did.

They'd been seen in the area. It was all I had. Fanny Black—Skip or Scott—and Carol.

That first night I didn't get anywhere. I felt the blues coming on and it only made me tense. A woman would have been the answer, something soft and warm and understanding. Someone who could see past the bags under my eyes and the dirty whiskers and unkempt hair. Someone who could see the man through the mess.

I got to the office at around three that night, opened a bottle of beer and played my tape machine. There was a message from Rufus, another THREAT from a crazy-ass bitch named Rita—she was still after my blood, wanted to see me either dead or castrated because I just plain got tired of making it with her. It's a long story I won't go into—except to say the stench of her cunt was definitely a decisive factor in that little drama, not to mention the mole and warts on her butt. Moles and warts on butts turn me off.

The tape played on. There was Rita again. Shit. A third message was from a former client (female) who wanted to get together and have intercourse. Exact word she used: "*intercourse.*" "And maybe some oral copulation," the voice added. Hell, I had to smile. She said her name was Grace. I couldn't place her. If it got bad enough I could call her.

There was a ruckus outside. Two drunks were beating up on a transvestite. I shut the machine off and called out to them. The drunks ignored me and continued pounding away at the transvestite. I whistled loud and let them see the .38. I aimed. It didn't make any difference. I don't think they were able to see that far. I re-holstered the .38, grabbed the metal ball bat, and scrambled down the flight of stairs. Those motherfuckers. They want to kick someone's ass, let them kick mine.

I reached the corner across the street and the dirtbags took off. The transvestite kept thanking me and wouldn't stop.

"It's all right," I said.

The transvestite offered to blow me. I returned to the office. It was too late to call Rufus. Bars closed at two. I would have to make it a point to give him a ring tomorrow. I returned to the apartment, read some Derek Raymond and slept.

I recognized the milkman's knock a few hours later. He had my quart of milk, the cottage cheese, the eggs and OJ. I thanked him and closed my eyes and not until I looked down to see that I was naked as a jay-fucking-bird did it explain the funny look the milkman had had on his face.

I was groggy, in pretty bad shape. I'd had only four hours sleep. I left the stuff in the refrigerator and returned to bed. I had an erection. Me and that goddamn erection. I was sick of it. Always hard. I got in the shower, swallowed some OJ, dressed and went out.

A clear, smogless day. I headed in the direction of MacArthur Park and the generally crappy area of town that my office was located in. The drunks were all over the place, sleeping. They couldn't sleep at night, not unless they wanted to chance getting shanked, so they dozed during the day: on benches, in doorways, on people's lawns. There was one taking a leak in the alley as I walked past. I recognized him but kept walking and didn't say anything. I had a headache and I was in a bad ass-kicking mood. I didn't particularly like being this way—and when the mood, this kind of blue/gray mood strikes, it is rare.

By the time I reached the office on Sixth, the air had cleared up my head and I felt a lot better. I wanted a woman, and I was on a case. Fanny Black, Lloyd Black, Skip or Scott and Carol. I was still hard down there. It's a curse, when 90 percent of the time all you can think about is getting laid, when your dick just won't stay down. The cocksucker would do me in some day. Heart attack right in the middle of the act. I don't think I'd want to go out that way. Some say "what a way to go." But I say bullshit to that. I'm not afraid of buying it. When it comes I'll take it, but not like that (preferably not like that), because I'd want a second ride.

I made it up the flight of stairs. Reached the hallway and recognized the woman standing outside my office door. She was two inches taller than me, a large woman, sad looking, the tip of her nose gone—and I never could figure out how the hell it might have happened. For some inexplicable reason, every time I see her there is this strange image of a hot iron being either flung at her nose or pressed against it. It's a freaky image. But how the hell does someone's nose get like that? The tip just gone—like someone had come along and chopped it off. She wasn't a bad fuck, as I remembered, but I don't go in for repeaters (as I have stated before). I wasn't interested.

"Hi, Grace."

"I want you to do something for me, Felix." She was one of the few who called me by my first name. Usually it's Choo-Choo, or it's Mr. Buschitski. Some call me just plain Buschitski, because they like the sound of it. I didn't care, so long as their checks didn't bounce (the rare times I accepted a check).

"I'm seeing someone," I lied.

"It's not that. I need you to find someone."

As I proceeded to unlock my door on the north side of this hallway, the private dick's door directly across my me opened, and the trio: a middle-aged, ragged-looking, unshaven Woody Putsky appeared with a couple of snarling pit bulls on leashes, followed by Ilsa Goth, a bigger-than-life, half-Danish/half Swiss uber babe with auburn hair followed, then the third dude, about half Putsky's age, who went by Doc Holiday followed her. They usually gave me the air. Noses up; they were too good to so much as acknowledge me. Never would let me in on a case even when they needed some help. Didn't think I was good enough to be associated with. Fuck 'em, I thought. Holiday locked the door behind them, and they were gone.

"Who's that?" asked Grace.

"Losers," I said. Entered my office. She followed me in.

"You know our policy around here: once we solve your case, that's it. Don't come back. We don't want to see you again. I know it sounds indifferent, cold, heartless, whatever you want to call it—and it's nothing personal (yes, it is: *not the same bullshit twice*), that's just a rule we have around here."

"Who's we?" she said. "You got a partner now?"

"Basically, I operate alone."

"So who's we?"

I sighed. "I use a backup man now and then." Reached back for a bottle of Coors in the fridge. I offered her one. She shook her head and fired up a butt.

"Would you fuck me?" she said. I was horny, like I said, but I had rules. I didn't want Grace in the picture again.

"I'm seeing someone, Grace."

"You? You don't believe in relationships, remember? Remember what you said—ever since that woman—what's her name?—left you."

"It was mutual," I said.

"Beside the point." Then she said: "Forget it. I never begged a man to fuck me before in my whole life."

"I got crabs, Grace," I said. Thought to scratch my nuts just then.

"Do you?" she asked.

I nodded.

"In that case—right. We're better off not to do anything."

She left.

The phone rang.

Lloyd Black was inquiring about his sister. I told him I needed more money before I could proceed. He promised to drop by later that day with the balance. I asked him to call before he did and hung up. I pulled on the beer. Cars were honking outside. It was bumper to bumper. I stood and looked out the window. There were crowds everywhere. The deli across the street was packed, MacArthur Park across the way was crowded as well: picnickers and panhandlers. It was one of the busiest and probably poorest intersections in the city—but every now and then you could see people smiling. Good weather had that effect on some folks, in spite of hard-to-ignore poverty.

The phone rang.

"You bastard!" the female voice at the other end screamed. It was Rita. "You lousy stinking bastard."

"Me? Stinking? Why don't you wash your cunt once in a while. It would help, you know."

"Would you see me if I did?"

"I doubt it."

"I'll see to it you get your nuts cut off."

I yawned. "It's been tried."

"You're a lousy lay, Buschitski. You think you're hot shit! You don't know how to eat pussy, you can't fuck—"

"That why you keep calling?"

"Be nice to me, damn you. . . ."

She was weeping.

"Listen to me, Rita honey, you got a good man there in Manny. Stay with him. He needs you." The guy was a lush and he preferred young boys.

"There was a time when he wanted me, Choo-Choo," she said. "Don't know what's gotten into him. . . ."

"Understanding, Rita," I said. "Try a little understanding. Show him you really care." I hung up.

No more answering the goddamn phone for the remainder of the day. She needed a shrink. I'm not a goddamn shrink. She needs shock therapy. How the hell am I gonna give her shock therapy? I must have been drunk the night I fucked her; I must have been out of my skull. The phone was ringing and I could hear her voice being picked up on the tape. I left the office. I'd had enough.

I walked into a bar around the corner. They had a color set up there hanging from the ceiling. I was an Angels fan. The Angels were losing to a lesser team: Milwaukee. The Angels weren't going to the World Series. I turned my back to it and got a beer and a bag of pretzels from Homer the barkeep. A finger tapped me on the shoulder. Norbert. He had a crew cut like Rufus, same mustache. Lot of these gay guys look alike. Norbert was a gay writer, porno. He wanted to present me with a copy of his latest. I read the title: *THE MAN WHO LIKED DICK.* I'd worked on a case for Norbert two years back, located a runaway lover in Sausalito. Norbert said he was making money as a writer. I asked how the love affair was going.

"We split up," Norbert said. "That's what *THE MAN WHO LIKED DICK* is about. My mate wanted to play the field. What could I do?"

He excused himself to go to the john. I glanced up at the color tv. Milwaukee was winning. No way the Angels would be able to catch up. Four to three Brewers. Top of the ninth. The Angels struck out. That was all she wrote. The Brewer fans were on their feet going crazy. And all the guys in the bar kept saying: "Shit, the Angels are a better team. Milwaukee got lucky is all."

I finished off my beer and took a drive to Hollywood, cruised west along the boulevard and kept my eyes open. I spotted the old lady and her dog near the *Hungry Tiger* restaurant on LaBrea. I got out, asked her if she needed any money. She shook her head, and showed me a bunch of change in her hand. She wondered if I might go in and buy her a cup of coffee. She didn't want to go inside herself. I didn't take her change, went in and bought the coffee and had a couple of questions to ask her.

"I haven't seen them since," she said.

I drove on toward the Strip. When I reached Fairfax, I dipped south on it to Santa M., took it west all the way to Holloway and basically covered the same ground I had the night before. The sun was out, it was still a pleasant day, and it kept the night owls away. It scared them. I would have to do it again after the sun went down.

I circled, and took it east on Santa Monica Boulevard and stopped at Danny's Dogs, got a medium steak sandwich with a pineapple Bang and ate with the other freaks and losers. Some of the teens had multi-colored hair, some of the males had earrings dangling from earlobes.

Not until I was nearly through eating did it dawn on me to ask the Korean short order cook. (*Some private dick.*) He looked at the photo.

"Ha'd to say," he said in pidgin English. "Ha'd to say. Many people come. All look same to me."

We both laughed at that.

Then he nodded pensively. "Maybe; maybe yes—"

"Was a white chick with her? Tall guy with blond hair?"

"Yes yes. I pretty sure."

That was it. I wasn't any closer.

He indicated the trailer there on the corner to his left. I looked. The trailer had been recently placed there. It was full of video games for the kids to use. "They here," he said. "This morning almost all night I think. After they eat. Play video game."

I thanked him. The winds were picking up a bit and I had to finish off my meal in the Caddy. Video games, huh? Maybe they'll be back.

I dialed Rufus's number from a pay phone. He wasn't in yet. It was 1:00 in the p.m., the bar wouldn't open until around five or six. I went in the *Pussycat Theatre* to kill some time. There was a lot of hot fucking and sucking going on up on that screen. And I needed to taste some pussy bad, real bad. I was even considering calling Grace, missing nose tip and all. Maybe even loony, suicidal Rita.

They had a former lingerie model up there being fucked by two guys—and she was young and good looking. Plenty of ass. One guy was sliding a big thing of a boner in and out of her shaved cunt, while another guy, hung like a mule, slid it in and out of her lipstick-glistening red lips. I couldn't take it and left.

There are times in this business when things will happen, just fall out of the blue, like a much-needed clue materializing, for instance, just like that; or a witness confessing, just like that; or a corpse surfacing, just like that. Only none of these things happened on this case. I needed to get more money from this guy Lloyd Black. I don't work for free. Choo-Choo Buschitski ain't no sucker—and I had a feeling this guy Black thought I might be one.

I dialed my office number, and using my gizmo was able to play back my messages. Rita again. There was a message from Black that he was coming by at three, and then another message from Black that he had slipped my money under my door in an envelope (because I hadn't been there to take it).

I drove to the office. There was an envelope there with forty bucks in it—only now I needed another hundred. I got expenses. I dialed Black's number. Nobody answered. I looked down. My dick stayed up there. Rufus picked up the phone at his end on the third ring.

"Where ya been, Buschitski?" he said. "I been calling and calling."

"Lay it on me, babe."

"They were in here after you split last night . . . and they're here now."

"Good."

"Only thing is the black chick's not with them."

"Thanks, Rufus," I said, and hung up.

I was parking my Cadillac outside the bar in less than twenty-five minutes. A tall blond dude, early thirties, wearing a straw cowboy hat, walked to a Chevy station wagon with a white chick. I hurried inside. I told Rufus what I had just seen outside. He nodded.

"That was them, babe," he said.

I hurried back out.

The Cowboy Hat and the chick were pulling away in the wagon. It took me about two blocks in my Caddy to catch up. They were headed east on Santa Monica.

They went north on Vine, took it to Hollywood and drove farther east, all the way to Vermont. The station wagon made a left turn, a short while later another left. And finally ended up stopping in some alley.

The girl got out and went into the courtyard. The cowboy stayed in the station wagon. A short while later the woman reappeared with a man casually dressed. They got in the Chevy wagon and drove off. I stayed with the wagon for about a mile. It seemed to be going back in the same direction, maybe returning to the bar. What the hell was going on? I wanted to find out what was inside that house—and I had to piss (even more so than I wanted to taste pussy).

There was a gas station nearby. I took a long leak and returned to the house. I looked around—and didn't like the setup because it made me feel like a Peeping Tom. (Peepers tended to get shot.) Mariachi music blasted from one or two of the apartments—and maybe the families had decided to combine the apartments in some sort of ritual celebration. A husband and wife were fighting and screaming at each other from a third apartment. Glass was being shattered. A baby cried nonstop.

I remained standing. Not knowing what to do or where to start. There were two apartments on my right, two on my left—add a second floor to that. It was a small court, and a noisy one. There was a tv going, someone was watching a boxing match, another set, going full blast, had some kind of news program on.

I climbed the steps. A woman weeping came through faintly, I was sure of it. As I neared the door, the cowboy and the other guy were both back.

"The fuck you think you're doing, sonny?" the cowboy said.

"Who? Me?" was my clever response.

The other guy seemed mild-mannered and insisted he didn't want any trouble.

"No trouble, no trouble at all," the cowboy assured him. "No sense trying to break into that place, boy," the cowboy was saying to me. "Ain't nothing there. My place."

I nodded. Fine. Great. I wanted him to open that door because I wanted a look-see inside. He got a key out, unlocked the door. The weeping was easily discernible now.

"What chu waitin' on?" the cowboy said with a half-grin or half something. I didn't need a telegram from Western Union to tell me the cocksucker was armed—so I didn't bother with my own piece. He would have beaten me to the draw probably (being a cowboy and all).

I used my favorite and most efficient method of reasoning with dirtbags like this: I sent a hard fist into the big man's jewels. He dropped to one knee, reaching for his shoulder rig. I had mine out already and aimed at his Adam's apple. I looked; the other guy had pissed his pants. He wondered if he might be able to leave. I reached for his gun.

"Let's go," I said. Motioning both of them inside the apartment. There was very little furniture to be seen. A worn sofa, used tv, a kitchen table with two chairs. The girl sitting in a corner of the sofa was the girl in the photo—only what I was looking at was bleeding from her nose and mouth. She were welts; her blouse was torn. I couldn't tell exactly how old she was and guessed her to be in her early twenties. She was looking at the gun in my hand and wiping her nose with a white hanky.

The cowboy had recovered quite well. Nobody had to explain what was going on: the guy in the wet pants was a trick, the cowboy a pimp, and Fanny Black was either a hooker or being forced into it. I had no idea what Lloyd Black's role was in all this. He could have been her brother. I wasn't sure. The cowboy went for a knife he had hidden inside one of his boots. Another kick sent him reeling against the tv, shattering the picture tube and knocking him almost senseless. I picked up the knife.

"What's Lloyd Black to you?" I asked the girl. She had no idea what I was talking about. I asked her name.

"Fanny Black," she said. I described the guy in the purple suit. She knew who I was talking about.

"What's going on here?" I said. "Can you talk? You want out of here? What?"

There were glasses near the sink. I got one. Rinsed it out, filled it with water and handed it to her. She drank it down. More tears flowed. She'd been beaten pretty bad.

"Who hit you?" I asked.

Her gaze was fixed on the cowboy. "Why don't you talk to me?" I said. "I'm not clear on everything. I'm a private investigator. I was hired to find you by this guy in a purple suit."

She cleared her throat.

"Take me away from here," she pleaded. I helped her to her feet and walked her down the steps. I got a little more information out of her. The guy in the purple suit was her ex. When she left him she had no place to stay and ended up with the cowboy and his hooker.

I asked Fanny if she wanted to press charges against the cowboy. She shook her head. She just wanted to get back home to New York and her family. I told her what her ex had said about wanting to leave LA by the end of the month. I asked her if she would consider calling him, that he was worried about her.

I drove her to a pay phone and watched her dial the number I had been given. Then I drove her to Winchell's, the same one where I had met her boyfriend that night. He was there. She rushed to him. He had his arms wrapped around her in a hard embrace. I think I had a lump in my throat. Hell, it reminded me of that chick, you know the one? Four years ago. But that's supposed to be forgotten, so I can't think about it. . . .

The guy looked at me. "Thank you," he said.

"You're welcome," I said. "By the way," I added, "what is your name?"

"Jerry," he said, smiling. "Jerry Crenshaw. Me and my lady here . . . well, we had split up . . . and I didn't think she'd want anything to do with me afterwards, so I thought it might be best to give you another name—in case you caught up with her, so she wouldn't hate me for trying to find her. . . ." His eyes welled. He was looking down. Fanny squeezed him harder. I watched them walk down the street that way, arms around each other. I ordered a cup of decaf and a chocolate-covered doughnut and sat at a table. I had pussy on my mind.

Angel—the Crazy Woman
A PI Choo-Choo Buschitski Long Short

It's not one of my happier recollections. I was coming out of the blood bank that Friday morning (I had to give blood for money in order to get enough food to carry me through the weekend)—that's when Wolfram Chang come up out of nowhere, floored me with a two-by-four, got the seven bucks the blood bank had given me, and took off. I had the .32 out of the holster strapped to my calf, but I was way too groggy and weak to even seriously consider using it. Wolfram was Chinese, and I think he had some US Indian in him. Either way, the cocksucker was gone with my chow money. The private dicks you read about—Archer, Marlow, Spade, Hammer, etc., etc., etc., get cases up the ying-yang. It had been okay for me for a while too, but then "the recession" hit, and nobody could afford a private dick anymore. The attorneys weren't throwing any work my way (they liked the slicker, bigger outfits, I guess), and what did come my way I didn't take: hookers wanting their runaway suitcase pimps tracked down so that they could blow them away (with a firearm), or vice versa: pimps frothing at the mouth because "*that cunt ho*" had skipped town with two days' worth of jack in her purse. Some repeaters called. I wasn't interested. It's a self-destructive rule I have, but I was in a self-destructive mood. So be it. All I wanted was to catch up with Chang and beat his oversized head in.

Wolfram had turned me on to some healthy Asian pussy once (during his wrestling days at the Olympic Auditorium). He was always drunk, seldom trained, and the promoters quit using him. I did what I could toward the end of his career, pulled a string here and there, got him a match now and then, but after a while even I couldn't do anything for him. Wolfram Chang was 6'2" and ugly. He weighed 250 and had a ponytail down to his fat ass. He was a filthy pig of a man and I wanted his hide now. Because of the way he'd handled things, I had a migraine. My skull throbbed.

I got to my feet and staggered back inside the blood bank. They said I couldn't give anymore blood for a while. I nodded, sat down near the Kool-Aid table and had some of their pink Kool-Aid and cookies. I recognized some of the other drunks who stayed in the neighborhood. They recognized me as well. I kept my head down. I didn't want anything to do with anybody.

Goddamn Wolfram Chang.

I'm gonna piss on your worthless hide, Wolfram Chang, when I catch up with you.

I walked the two blocks to my office near Alvarado and climbed the flight of stairs. My refrigerator was empty. There was no beer. I wanted a beer. I reached down for the AnsaPhone and contemplated pawning it. I thought about selling and/or pawning one of my guns. I had, as mentioned, the .32 and I had a .38 (for bigger targets like Chang). I didn't want to start thinking about killing the dirtbag over what he'd done, but if he had walked through my door that instant I might have.

I turned the AnsaPhone on. That crazy cunt Rita was calling again. She was threatening suicide. When she's not threatening to do herself in, she's threatening to have my nuts. We fucked once. *One time.* We all have episodes in our lives we'd like to forget, nightmares we wish would go away. They seldom do.

Her message ended. *Only the second message was hers as well.* Different tone. She wasn't shouting. She was apologizing and saying that her boyfriend Manny was back. That was it. No more messages. The Kool-Aid and the cookies added to the nausea.

I stood facing the window. I thought about past clients——the Maggot Sisters. I know, I know, rough name—but that was only their stepfather's surname. They were a couple of gems. Sexy ladies. Two miracles. Then there was that hard bitch Celia, with a body that made your mouth water. And there had been others over the years. I'd had my share of luck. With my looks (*or lack of*), and unwillingness to bend to anybody else's way but mine, I would say I'd had more than my share of luck. And now, I was sick; sick of the business, sick of working in skid row, sick of the stench, sick of everything, including myself. I farted.

Wolfram Chang staggered in—wasted out of his moronic brain (*with my money*). He was grinning; a big shit-eating grin from ear to ear. He placed sixty-five cents on my desk. Leaned against it for support. He smelled. I moved away. Got closer to the fresh air coming in through the open window.

"I'm sorry, Choo-Choo," he stammered. "Needed a drink." He belched a couple of times. "Brought your money back," he said, spreading out the coins with his dirty fat fingers.

"*You fat fuck,*" was what came out of my mouth.

"Wanna hit me, Choo-Choo? Wanna hit me? Go ahead. . . . I won't do nothin'."

"Why would I want to hit you, Wolfram?" And I had a fist flying toward his bloated face that instant. It stunned him, just a bit. My knuckles were bleeding.

"Hit me again," he said. "Go ahead, Choo-Choo. Hit me again. I won't do nothin'. Go ahead."

The cocksucker probably thought I wouldn't hit him again. I knew him too well. He's got to learn to communicate with people other than with a two-by-four.

I got a towel out of the bottom drawer, wrapped it around the other hand, and let him have it with everything I had in me. That one worked a little better. Wolfram staggered back, crashing into the wall behind him. I was proud of myself. I still had it, even with a pint of blood drained out of me.

He didn't ask me to hit him again, but I did anyway. I had an idea: I wanted my next punch to send him back out of my office, and it did. Wolfram fell back into the hallway, landing on top of two mongrels who had been engaged romantically there. The dogs yelped, and took off. Wolfram couldn't get up.

"Next time you hurt me, you fat sack of dog shit," I told him, "I'm gonna make you really feel it—and I'm talking about hitting a homer off that brainless skull of yours!"

I'd gotten him a job at a car wash two weeks ago and he hadn't even been able to hold on to that. Brainless was right. Alkie mother.

I locked my door on the way out, made it outside to the pawnshop around the corner. I got twenty bucks for the smaller gun (and a receipt). Stretch, the pawnbroker (because we had done business before), gave me forty days to buy the piece back (if I still wanted it).

Wolfram was waiting outside. There was blood and dirt on his face.

"Buy me a drink, Choo-Choo," he said.

"Kindly eat shit, Wolfram, and die," I told him, and walked away.

So now I had money for gas, I had worked Wolfram over, and I should have felt a lot better—but I didn't. The Caddy was parked in front of the triple-X movie arcade. I reached the car, unlocked the door. A wino staggered up. He wanted money. Usually I didn't mind; this time and this day I wasn't giving *sweat*. He got indignant. "Ya think you're better, Buschitski? Ya think you're better? You're nothin'! Dirt! You're dirt!"

"Go blow mule dick, Fritz," I told him, started the Caddy up and pulled away.

I put five bucks worth in the tank at the nearest gas station. There was a pinball arcade not far from there. The place was half-full, mostly kids. I found a machine and played pinball.

I'd always thought of myself as a success. For years I had done (*always*), I thought, what I wanted to do—not much. I was a private dick with my own office, I had my own apartment, worked when I felt like it. I made rent, got laid now and then, kept the Fleetwood full of gas and running, and I masturbated. In my book, Felix "Choo-Choo" Buschitski's book, that was SUCCESS. Only now, I wondered. I was lost—felt that way. Maybe giving up that pint of blood was the cause (partly) behind the blues. I'd given blood before and never felt this shitty.

A vicious-looking thing in her forties bumped into my pinball machine, causing me to lose too many points. I think I called her a dirty whore, because she kicked me in the shins, then followed up by slamming me in the face with her purse. I was down on the floor. The purse must have had lots of change in it. Some nickels and dimes spilled out. I stayed under the pinball machine and she continued to kick with her feet. I was able to reach out from where I was at and yanked that purse away. I rose to my feet, held her at bay with my other hand. I pulled a roll of quarters out of the purse. I flung the purse at her. She kept looking at the rolled quarters in my fist and fled. I pocketed the quarters and proceeded to play pinball. Blood dripped from my forehead onto the glass of the pinball machine.

I wiped it away. It didn't work.

I went in the restroom, got some paper towels and dabbed at it, washed my face; got a paper towel and held it against the cut that way. Hell, I needed to get drunk.

Three six-packs and a bag of chips at a nearby liquor store cost me about eight bucks. The wild-eyed bitch with the purse was waiting for me when I came out.

"I'm sorry," she said.

I unlocked the door to my Caddy. "Can you suck dick?"

"I'd like to have a beer with you," she said.

"You fucking almost kill me and you want to have a beer with me?"

"You called me a whore."

"I guess I did."

"How about it?"

I looked at her. She was crazy, no doubt about it. She'd done some time in a mental home, I was willing to bet my beer and last dime on it—but she had legs, and most of all, she had a big ass.

"What's your name?" I asked, unlocking her side.

"Angel," she said, as she got in. "Just call me Angel."

I turned the key and drove. Thinking about jamming turkey neck down her throat and then maybe giving it to her in her ass got me plenty hard. She kept looking down at my erection and smiled. Like the true gentleman that I can be at times, I popped the top on one of the cans and handed it to her. She took a pull—then I placed her left hand over my groin. She kept rubbing gently. I finally had something to grin about. Could be part of the attraction was knowing she was nuts.

We got to my place and she headed straight for the john, dropped her skirt and took a crap, open door and all. She pulled on her can like that, shitting and farting. Hell, it turned me on. I got some classical music going on the radio, popped open two more cans and put the rest in the refrigerator.

I had clean sheets in the closet, but would save them for another occasion. I angled the bed so that I could watch her from it, then I stretched out across it, held my cock in my hand and pulled on the beer.

She flushed it away, then I heard her pissing some more, flushed that away and had the sense to take a shower. I was stroking my meat when she joined me in the bed. She had put the skirt and blouse back on.

"You don't have to take that off if you don't want to," I told her.

She smiled. "I got a scar," she said, indicating her waist, "that I didn't want you to see."

"I don't give a shit about that," I said, hiking up her skirt, and ran my hand up deep, up her thighs and pussy.

She had strong legs, the way waitresses her age sometimes do. The veins weren't bad. She rubbed my cock with cold fingers that made it even more sensitive, then she lowered her mouth over it. I played with her cunt, but then the pleasure got so great that I had to get up on my knees. I watched her work on it, looking up from time to time and grinning, those wild eyes going crazy. Then I jammed it in all the way and unloaded! She took it, knew enough to keep working the tongue and hand until there was nothing more to draw out. Hell, I bit my tongue. I dropped back against the pillow, eyes closed. She covered my balls and upper thighs with wet kisses, and when she was through with her beer, she asked if she might have another. I nodded, started to get up. She wouldn't let me and got it herself.

I opened the can for her, as she had long fingernails. She pulled on it, a good one. The wild eyes looked at me.

"Well?" she said.

"You're one of the best little cocksuckers I've ever known," I told her, not that there was anything little about her. She liked that.

"I'm not so good at fucking," she said.

"Let me be the judge."

"I got a big pussy," she said.

"Oh yeah?"

She pulled on the beer, shrugged. "That's what I've been told. That's how come I learned to give better head."

I drank my beer, turned up Stravinsky. There was no need to talk. She wanted to know about me. I told her what there was to tell. And when I didn't ask any questions, she offered answers just the same.

She had money, an inheritance, three grown kids, an ex-husband who was in prison (for what wasn't clear); her own mother had committed suicide when Angel was twelve, as did Angel's sister at age twenty-five. Her father had died of cancer four years back. She did a stretch in Camarillo. And she asked if I wanted to know her real name.

I shrugged.

She said it was Desdemona.

She wanted to know my name. I told her people who knew me called me Choo-Choo. That was all I told her. (I didn't want another Rita on my hands.)

They followed up Stravinsky with some Mozart, and that with DaPussy, er rather, Debussy. I was ready to go again. Desdemona (or

Angel) said she had to pee. She left the door open. And I watched.

When she returned I got her to bring out the Crisco cooking oil and had her rub it on my meat. I wanted the second time to be as good as the first. Angel (or Desdemona) got carried away with the oil and rubbed it over my upper thighs, my belly, and up toward my chest. I turned over with her help and she got my neck and back. She had strong hands and was able to apply the needed pressure to get at the tough shoulder and neck muscles. I was feeling better than I'd felt in a long time, then I heard her mumble something that sounded like:

"You pig. You fucking slime."

She was sitting up, frozen-faced, looking down at me *and not* looking at me. The eyeballs had gotten darker. Nobody lived there. *Oh shit*, I thought. *Here it comes. She's gonna go berserk on me.* She *rapped* me across the face with the bottle of oil, and tried for it a second time. I slapped it out of her hand, then backhanded her but good. She fell to the side, buried her face in the bedsheet and wept.

I got some of the oil off of me with the other sheet and felt the right side of my face: throbbing and lower lip swollen. Finally, she turned over on her back, staring at the ceiling like that, eyeballs frozen again.

"The fuck is the matter with you?" I said. "I know you're nuts, but Jesus Christ!"

"You just want to fuck me," she said. "You don't care about me. You don't care what happens to me."

"Bullshit," I said. "I do care—"

"No, you don't."

"To a certain extent I do."

After a moment, she said: "Well, to a certain extent, you might."

"Of course I do," I said. "The hell do you think I am?"

"You didn't want to know my name."

I had to laugh. "So what? Angel is nice. I like Angel."

"I told you my real name."

I got a beer. She reached out for it. I let her have a pull.

"You must meet lots of people," she said. "Being a snoop."

I shrugged. "Fuck all that."

"See? I was right. You're a bastard."

I sat down with a sigh. "Okay. . . . Sometimes it is exciting—and other times, mostly, it's bullshit. It's not what people think. All you got to do is take a look at what's out there."

She was looking at me.

"I'm talking about people. A bunch of lifeless motherfuckers, 90 percent. Dull—dull shit. I don't know what's causing it. Maybe it's tv, maybe it's the papers. Worries."

"You think I'm like that?"

"Like what?"

"Like them—dull?"

I was smiling. "You? Hell, you got balls—a lot of balls for a woman. There never was a woman who gave better head—and not many who even come close. And you know I mean it."

She liked that, and wanted more beer. I let her have the can. After she finished it off, the hand with all the oil on it was back rubbing my Johnson. I got some oil on my pussy finger and got it in her butt and smeared Crisco all over the rest of her muscled ass. I got some more oil up her asshole, then maneuvered her around so that she was on all fours and that large ass looking up at me. I got my cock inside her brown hole and slid it in slowly at first. I pulled back just as slowly and drove it in again, then found my rhythm and stayed with it. It was great. There was no need for speed. I felt everything there was to feel. Angel hadn't said anything; maybe her cunt WAS too big. Just the same, I withdrew it and got it inside her pussy. It wasn't that bad. I pumped a little faster and kept increasing speed and force. I hammered away, all the way each time, gave her everything I had. Her moans told me I was doing the right thing. She screamed my name. I got it in there one final time and held it. I shot JUICE!

After that, all I was interested in was sleep, and I wasn't about to close my eyes with her around. I didn't want to wake up with a knife sticking out of my ribs. She wanted to keep fucking. All I wanted was rest. She said up until now she'd been celibate for nine months. That she hadn't met any real men until I came along, that they all had been scared of her. Hell, they probably had more sense than I did, that's all.

Some of Act II of Tchaikovsky's *Swan Lake* came through on the radio. She kept talking through most of it. When it was over, we showered, dressed, and I took her to a restaurant near Vermont. She insisted on paying for it (as the beer had been on me). *I didn't stop her, or try to stop her, or pretend to try to stop her.* (CONFUSED LIBERATED MALE—SHIT. IN MY BOOK, THE ONE WHO HAS THE BUCKS PAYS FOR IT. Simple and easy.)

She talked about things through the meal. Sure, I listened and paid attention, but for the most part my head was somewhere else. Then she finally got around to her inheritance, and said I was different because I hadn't tried to pry it out of her, how much she had, etc.

"Look, Desdemona—" I told her.

"Angel."

"The reason I don't give a shit is because it doesn't concern me." I have never placed a whole lot of value on money. Could be why I was broke (most of the time).

"You're different," she said.

I shrugged. "I'm a bum, I know it—"

"No, you're not."

"I call them as I see them. I'm a bum because I like it that way—"

"Did you ever want to do anything else?"

"Maybe—maybe I did, and maybe deep down I always knew I'd never get it. And it's just as well. We all know what a dream come true can turn out to be, don't we?"

I think she understood more than I did. You wished and prayed for a dream to happen, and then it does—*it does happen*—and you realize it's a NIGHTMARE. I was tired.

"So what now?" she wondered.

I looked at my watch. "I got a client I have to meet."

"Can I go with?"

"No."

She was quiet.

"Why not?" she asked.

"Look, if you want to stay at my place, fine. I have to go see a client."

"You just want to dump me. You're seeing someone else."

"Bullshit. And what if *I were* seeing someone else? The fuck is that to you? I mean, Christ, we don't have anything going here. *We just met.*"

She stood up, red-faced, the jugular pumping blood. "If you think I am to be treated like some *cheap whore*—YOU GOT ANOTHER THING COMING!"

"Will you please calm down?"

"WHY SHOULD I? WE MADE LOVE; WONDERFUL, BEAUTIFUL LOVE, AND NOW I'M NOTHING BUT A CHEAP STRUMPET! YOU'RE A BASTARD!" she screamed. "BASTARD!"

All eyes were upon us. I stared back. The dirtbags looked away. I got enough money out of Desdemona's purse, left it there on the table to cover the meal and dragged her outside. When we reached the Caddy, she held on to me, sobbing. "Don't leave me, Choo-Choo; *please don't leave me. . ."*

The bastard in me was saying: drop the crazy woman—but I didn't have it in me to just leave her like this.

"They always leave me. . . ."

I had my arms about her waist.

"*They do, they always leave. . . . Even Pop . . . even Pop. . . . I know I'm not right in the head. . . . I know that. . . . God made me this way, I know he did. This is God's way. . . . I'll be a good woman to you, Choo-Choo. . . . I'll be good. Just take care of me. . . . I need a good man to take care of me.*"

I was the one clinging to her now. Something rushed up through my lungs, a ball of emotion that held in my throat and choked, then proceeded on up and came out through my eyes. Tears rolled silently down my face. More than anything, often (too often) we are messengers of pain. We know how to hurt, how to say: *No.* How to say: *Fuck off.* I'd had my share of being this way, and I'd had it done to me by enough women.

We drove back to my apartment in silence. When we got there, she dozed off almost immediately. I sat in a chair across from the bed. I had Chopin turned down low and listened to the music in the dark.

Walking Time Bomb

Frank Blair stared in the mirror. There wasn't much there. A twenty-eight-year-old loser stared back. *Nothing left to lose,* as the cliché goes. The nervous twitch in his left eye was beginning to annoy him. The job interview he was to make at 10:00 that morning forever on his mind. He'd been up all night thinking about it: the interview, the rent he was behind a month on now, the fourteen bucks he had to his name. Shit, fourteen fucking dollars. And the other day, at the unemployment office in West LA, they had told him: "Sorry, but no go. Fourteen is too much. Come back when you're down to three."

Jesus Christ, he couldn't believe it. *Come back when you're down to three?*

He'd tried getting food stamps. "Sorry," came back the answer. "We can't help you."

You can't help me? I've never drawn unemployment in my life. *I did a stint in 'Nam, you motherfuckers. I'm a vet.*

So what?

My rent is overdue.

Fuck you.

Right, baby, he thought. Fuck you, Frank Blair. Fuck you. You're dog shit. We don't hire dog shit around here. And he'd been getting that for eight years now. Oh, he'd gotten by on nothing menial work and jobs that didn't last. Temporary; they were always temporary. He'd walk into a company's hiring office, a place where wages were a bit higher than minimum, where at least potential for growth seemed possible, a way and a chance to get somewhere in life and the response was usually: "Sorry. Nothing available."

You're a trained killer. No use for killers back in the USA. Try being a mercenary, Frank Blair. Right. . . . You're dead inside, baby, and that's the way you'll remain—and that leaves one avenue of employment: killing.

Killer for hire. . .

He turned away from the mirror. Enough staring at the pitiful face. The room was small. Bed, chair, battered dresser. An end table with a lamp on it. Cheap, old, worn. Carpet was no different. This they called *furnished.*

He thought he might like to masturbate again—and he knew he could never do it right away, not this soon. He'd been pulling on it all night. That's what the hermit does to pass the time: he plays with himself, dreams about having someone to love, someone who would care about him.

There was a woman several years back, but she had dropped him after six months. His screaming in the middle of the night had been too much for her, the nightmares, the sleepwalking. He had tried to explain that it would all go away eventually, that he'd be all right; he would be just like everyone else, that it took time—to no avail. She had walked. She'd had too much sense to stick around with an unemployable loser.

Yeah, Blair, he thought, she was right. She sure was. "You'd be better off dead."

He glanced at the clock: 9:30. He got into the army fatigue jacket, dug his hand into one of the pockets for the switchblade and pressed the lever. The shiny steel blade swung out, clicking into place. Frank Blair held it, just held it like that. The cool, all-metal hilt felt good in his hand. Fine piece of craftsmanship. He recalled the day he'd purchased it just outside Ft. Polk upon his return from 'Nam, and he had carried it with him ever since. You never knew when you might have to defend yourself. Shit had a way of hitting the fan when you least expected it.

He folded the blade. Returned it to the right-hand pocket. He tried to picture the type of dork in the three-piece suit who would probably interview him, give him the bullshit, and finally tell him that he was not their type. He wondered if he'd be able to get through the interview without doing something stupid or embarrassing, something crazy. Interviews were anathema, always, all interviews. But Christ, he would have to get through it. That's all there was to it. Stay calm, collected, he thought. Act like you're okay. It's just another job interview. And just think if they hire you—sure, it's only a position in the mail room, but think of it—the convenience. *Just four blocks from where you live.* You wouldn't have to take the fucking LA bus, the nightmarish LA bus. You could walk to work—every day. Just walk. And so what if you're twenty-eight? They might give you a break. They might. You could be a pretty good mail clerk. Sure. You could do it. Only if they'd give you a chance.

He paused at the window, taking in the hamburger joint across the street, all those people eating their thick burgers, french fries; drinking their Cokes. He wished he could take a chance with the cash he had left and buy a hamburger. Only there was no way of telling that he had the job and instead of buying a hamburger, he might have to buy something that cost less and would last a lot longer. Rice. He would get a bag of rice later, rice and maybe a stick of butter or a bottle of catchup.

He stepped into the tiny closet-like space, opened the mini refrigerator. The two carrots were still there, the two hot dogs. The nearly empty jar of pickle relish.

I'll have one of the hot dogs for lunch when I get back, he thought. And maybe buy a soft drink to wash it down with. He closed the refrigerator door, reached for his sunglasses, put them on and went outside. He walked south on San Vicente to the high-rise on Wilshire. The sun was hot on his face. The sweat poured. His hands remained dug inside the pockets of his army jacket.

The beautiful women were everywhere in their high heels and sexy dresses, and not one looked at him. They didn't have to. He knew the score. Losers you can smell a mile away. But he couldn't help it, he wondered what if one, *just one* were to wrap her arms around him, *only one*, and told him how much she loved him, that she was so proud of him, to have someone like him . . . one woman to take to a movie or the park for a picnic or a walk . . . but he knew he was dreaming.

It's a dream, Frank Blair. Things like that don't happen to guys like you. Forget it.

He entered the building. The elevator was a smooth ride to the eighth floor. Not that he really wanted to take his protection off, but he got out of the jacket and took the dark glasses off as the door opened. It was a thick, burgundy-colored carpet that he walked across to a desk in the center of this huge room with many other desks and women walking around and smelling great and looking great and indifferent. You don't exist, Frank Blair. . . . I know . . . I know. . . .

He was given a form to fill out. He did. Returned it to the desk. He found a seat at one of the sofas. The others waiting to be interviewed were in three-piece suits. They were used to it. He felt out of place. Sweat poured down his neck.

There were huge white clocks all over the place, and they all had 10:20. One by one, the three-piece suits were interviewed. Frank leafed through the publications available: *Newsweek, Fortune, Wall Street Journal.* He kept looking up to check the time. After 11:00, Frank wondered if this asshole was ever going to see him? Finally, the secretary instructed him that the man would see him now.

Frank walked into the office. It was just like the countless other offices he'd been in, offices that had made him sweat, made him wish he were somewhere else. There was the large desk, the plaques on the wall behind it, the leather-bound volumes, the phone, framed photos of the guy's wife and kids: boy and girl.

The man stayed on the phone for ten minutes, all the while studying Frank's application before him. When he was through yakking on the phone, he looked up and told Frank that he was really too old for the job, that they were looking for someone younger, and that, in fact, the position had been filled.

"I'm sorry," the man said as he rose to his feet.

Frank thought about tearing him apart. You make me wait two hours to tell me the position has been filled? *You fucking asshole.*

"We got your number," the man said. "We'll let you know if something comes up."

Slowly, in something like a numb state, Frank Blair walked out of the office, walked the endless distance to the elevator. Sweat poured, the skull pounded. He punched a button for the elevator to come up. When the door opened, Frank did not get on. Instead, he turned and, taking his time, made it back to the office.

The sack of shit who had just interviewed him had been about to light a cigarette when Frank's switchblade sliced his neck open. Blood spurted. Frank kept jabbing the blade into the three-piece suit's chest and belly until he was too exhausted to continue. The shocked, in denial figure in the three-piece slid down to the blood-soaked carpet, gasping as he did. Finally, he was quiet.

Frank waited a moment to compose himself. One goddamn thing he was sure of: he felt better. Killing the cocksucker had made him feel a lot better. He wiped the blood from his hands, put the army jacket on to conceal his blood-stained shirt, and walked back to the elevator. This time when the door opened he got on. The Muzak made him feel like whistling. He whistled. And pretty soon he was singing softly the marching song they had taught him in basic: *"Ain't no use in goin' home—Jody got our gal and gone. Ain't no use in goin' back—Jody got our Cadillac. Ain't no matter what we do, Jody doin' our sister, too."*

He hummed and/or whistled the different variations of the tune on the way to Fatburger up the street on San Vicente. When he got there, he ordered a double cheeseburger with everything, large order of french fries with ketchup and a large Dr Pepper.

The Case of the Vengeful Vixen
A Choo-Choo Buschitski PI Episode

The trouble with a roach motel is having to figure out how to get the mothers to **check in**. *They're too smart for it.* Believe me. I had one motel sitting on top of the office refrigerator and one in back of it (the sightings of many roaches). I wasn't against using roach spray, as that seemed to be the only sure way of getting them, but I was expecting a client to show up any minute and refused to use the *Raid*. It was dusk outside. I had only left the one lamp on on my desk (in order to draw more of the bastards out). I could see three or four down by the roach motel in back of the refrigerator, but they wouldn't go in. They just kept circling the motel. THEY REFUSED TO GO INSIDE! Once, I'd caught it on tv, *their* roach motels (in the commercial) worked like magic. The roaches marched right on in there—and never came out.

There were three dead roaches in the motel on top of the refrigerator. The motel on the floor had none. NONE! One of the roaches climbed up on top of the motel. I picked up the motel and kept manipulating it, trying to get the roach to go in; I wanted to see the muther GO INSIDE AND DIE. The cocksuckers were driving me crazy. THIS WAS MY OFFICE, NOT THEIRS. WHAT FUCKING RIGHT

DID THEY HAVE TO FUCK WITH MY LIFE! The roach took a leap, and landed on the floor. He disappeared behind the refrigerator before I could get to him. The others were gone as well.

THAT'S IT! I'VE HAD ENOUGH! I'm getting the spray can out! I grabbed the *Raid* and *Black Flag* both. The door opened. She was in a full-length mink coat. The hair was long and black. I had no idea what her face looked like because she was wearing a Halloween mask. *What gives?* She opened the mink. The bitch was naked and she was built.

The fuck is going on here?—I wondered. She stood there, in heels, dragging on a butt.

"Hello, Choo-Choo. . ."

I couldn't place the voice. But I didn't care. My dick was hard and I moved toward her. I tried to reach for the mask, but she backed away; didn't want me to do that. Fine, I thought. My next move had me rubbing her cunt. I had lowered my head down to about her belly button when the blow to the back of my head laid me out on the decades-old linoleum. The cocksucker knew how to hit. I was seeing and hearing things—not unlike being inside a dark tunnel with intermittent lights flashing off and on in the distance. Couldn't make too much out. Maybe the roaches were laughing at me. I was finally getting mine for all the shit I'd put *them* through.

After a while, I got to my knees. A cowboy boot came up into my belly and sent me reeling back into my desk. That time the woman in the mask was laughing. Saliva poured from my mouth. Damn. I had always dreaded something like this happening someday. And that day had come. But did they know who they were fucking with? Did they have any idea that they were toying with *Felix "Choo-Choo" Buschitski?* That was my warning put to them: "You're messing with Felix 'Choo-Choo' Buschitski," I said.

"You're a fuck-up," I heard the woman say. "One big fuck-up."

The boot came again, between my nuts that time. I wished I was one of the motherfucking roaches. Bile, mixed-in with saliva came up, a river of it. The gloved hands lifted me off the floor—and I waited for it. I looked at the face that was doling out the punishment through blurry eyes. I was looking at some large white laughing teeth, a wart-covered nose, dark glasses. The nightmare was bald and tanned and smelled of Coppertone.

I saw the fist coming and closed my eyes. *POWWWW!* I never knew a man to fly so well. I was staring at a corner and some dead roaches and smelled *Raid* from the night before. Blood oozed out of my mouth this time.

You're a tough son of a bitch, I said to myself. You'll handle it. Get up, get up. You've got a .32 in the rig on your ankle, and a .38 in your shoulder holster. *Use them. OR ONE, AT LEAST! COME ON, YOU SON OF A BITCH! COME ON, FELIX!*

He lifted me up again, and dropped me in the trash can, head first. I was allowed a rest period while they both laughed about it. I heard skinhead pull out my chair behind the desk and sit in it. The woman's heels walked toward me. She was directly above me. I heard a trickle. The lousy bitch was pissing on me. I may have liked to have done it to a cunt or two in my time—but I didn't like it being done to me. No way. None of this *"golden showers"* bullshit.

I pretended I liked it. I could see skinhead was enjoying it as he stroked his meat. At least he was relaxed. Both were amused by the show.

I got my right hand down around my left ankle, unfastened the strap. I wrapped my fingers around the handle of the piece, took a deep breath and spun in the skinhead's direction and I unloaded four rounds into his ugly fat face. His body jerked a few times. Blood covered the desk and floor, then his body dropped to the side and continued to drop and landed on top of the paper sacks full of empty beer cans and bottles.

The bitch stiffened up. I rose to my feet. She was biting her lower lip. I was wiping blood from mine. I got the mink off of her and wiped my face in it.

"That's a three-thousand-dollar mink," she said.

I thought about ripping the Halloween mask from her face and for some reason didn't; maybe I was afraid to see what she really looked like. I let her keep the mask on, and locked the door. Then I pulled the shade down.

"You like golden showers, bitch? In that case, let's have a little more." I got my pecker out, and pissed on the coat, then I turned the stream on her.

I got it on her hair, her tits, the rest of her body. When I was through pissing, I thought about jamming my meat down her throat, but didn't have the nerve; she might have taken a bite.

I propped her up on the desk, and got a finger in there. She was wet. My cock was ready, and I drove it on in. She was tight. It was a good ride. I wanted another go, preferably in her ass, before I yanked that fucking mask off.

I got a tube of lube out and had her rub some of it on my cock. That got me half hard. I slid some of that stuff up her butt. Then I sat back in the chair, had a beer, while she continued to stroke my dick. The bottle was empty, and I was ready again.

"All right, bitch. Get over here," I told her. "Bend over."

She did.

"Get your hands on the edge of the desk for support." She was quite obedient. "That's fine, real fine."

There was lots of dark hair on her asshole, which excited me even more. I rubbed her pussy for a while, then got my cock in her butt, hard, all the way; damn near lifted her clean off the floor.

"You like that, ho? Huh? You like that?"

She didn't say anything.

"Who's laughing now, huh, cunt? You and your goddamn golden showers. Nobody pisses on Choo-Choo Buschitski and gets away with it. Nobody."

I gave her twenty good strokes, and finished. I needed a moment to rest up, then reached out and ripped the mask off. I wanted to puke. Nausea hit me. I'd never seen a face so disfigured. Christ.

"You bastard. . . . You happy now?" Her eyes welled. "*You bastard.*"

The voice sounded familiar. I couldn't place her. There was nothing about the face that made any sense to me: no eyebrows, tiny holes for a nose, a twisted mouth—and it was all a pinkish/yellow discoloration.

"ARE YOU HAPPY NOW, YOU FUCKING BASTARD?!?"

I didn't answer. None of it made any sense. There was a dead body in my office and I was sure someone must have heard those shots. The cops were going to have to be notified pretty damn soon.

"Why don't you tell me who the fuck you are?" I finally said out of anger and disgust. She'd had a heavy dose of bad luck, no doubt about it, but the bruiser had done a pretty good job of turning me into lean ground and damn near stopped my clock altogether. Then it clicked. Rita. Crazy, suicidal Rita. We'd had an affair about four years back. We had split (my decision), and she'd been threatening (off and on) to either have my balls cut off or to have me killed.

She wasn't looking at me now, she was looking down at the floor.

"I set fire to myself," she said. She pulled the wig off. The rest of the skin covering her head was in just as sorry shape. I almost wept for her, for all of us. . . . Instead, I picked up the phone and dialed.

"You should have done what I did"
A Cash Register Taxicab Trip

I'd been at the Plaza cab stand since 3:00 a.m. At five past six, the intercom blares: "We need a cab at the Tower, please. One taxi at the Tower."

I wipe sleep from my eyes. Ah, finally. A fare. All right. Maybe we can get the day moving, make rent, all that.

I pull away slowly, passing the Plaza entrance on my way up and over to the Tower, where the Reagans stay when in town, the Century City Tower, where the night before many limos had sat parked with hundreds of celebrities, plenty world famous, who had attended a benefit given to director Marty Scorsese. This is the same hotel where the president of Poland Lech Walesa is staying.

So I pull up to the door. Four college ballplayer types walk right past me and get in the cab station wagon already sitting there (he may have dropped a fare, more than likely), the tallest saying: "We'll take this wagon. We can get more people in the station wagon. There's two other guys coming down. They're stuck in the elevator I think."

I nod, okay; as long as I can get a decent fare out of this. I've got my lease on my mind ($180) that I need to pay for the use of the cab, gas, etc. I'm standing there with my trunk open and the bellhop wheels a pile of dark, garbage type plastic bags out loaded with stuff, a battered suitcase—and I hear a woman, cursing. She's swearing pretty damn loud. I look. A short, black woman in a dirty T-shirt, dirty sweatpants. On the heavy side.

"Don't give me your shit, you hear? I want some goddamn service! That's all I want! Gimme service! You won't gimme my ride, gimme service then, goddammit!"

I have no idea what the fuss is about. A second bellhop, skinny, in his forties, joins the other guy. They appear flustered, not knowing what to do, where to go with this woman and her belongings. Woman was being 86'd. It didn't take a Bobby Fischer to add this one up. I'm secretly hoping they don't put her in my cab. And it has nothing to do with race, believe me. This woman is a mess. She is either drunk or effed-up on dope.

The bellhops look my way. Both of them, looking at me. *No no no. Don't do that. Please.*

"My fare is coming down," I explain, throwing it out there. Never mind that my fare took off in the station wagon. And that line that guy gave me about someone being stuck in the elevator was pure crock. I'm too damn old and too weary to have to deal with another nutcase this early in the morning—and I also know I have to use caution and diplomacy. One has a right to turn down a fare now and then, for good reason, but if a cabbie becomes known for it at these hotels, what they do is make a little phone call—and suddenly you are no longer able to work said hotel.

The woman keeps cursing, making a fuss, drawing attention. And I see the inevitable coming. Right there and then I should have closed my trunk and got out of there—but no, it's a tricky situation, made more difficult by the fact the woman is black.

"So you're racist on top of everything else. You're fired."

Well, I didn't want that. And so they dumped the woman's junk—shampoo bottles, salt shakers, hair brushes, combs, lipstick, nail polish, hand lotions, perfumes, etc., in my trunk. All of it. A nice—not so little—pile.

She climbs in my backseat.

"Forty-two seventy-two Liemert," she says. Only she's mumbling and I can't figure out what she is talking about. I keep asking her to repeat it, and she does—but I still can't figure out what it is she's saying. Then she screams:

"JUST GO! DRIVE! MOVE IT! I don't have time for this."

I pull out of the driveway.

"Go right," she says. I do. "What you do is turn right on Motor," she tells me. Well, first we have to go to Pico—take that to Motor, but if you turned right on Motor off of Pico that would take you into 20th Century Fox, the motion picture studio.

"You mean turn left, don't you?"

"YOU HEARD WHAT I SAID: TURN RIGHT ON MOTOR!"

"We can't do that. You mean left, don't you?"

"DID YOU HEAR WHAT I SAID? I TOLD YOU TO TURN RIGHT! GODDAMMIT, I WANT YOU TO TURN RIGHT ON MOTOR! TURN RIGHT!"

I nod my head. Man, I really did it this time, screwed up good. I shouldn't have taken her. I should stop my cab right here on Avenue of the Stars and take all her stuff out of my trunk, and leave her here. Or else get her to the nearest cop car. I've done that before, had to. But then you've got the racism thing. Not only that, if you made a move like that, who is to say she might not totally explode? Keep your wits, stay calm; take her where she wants to go. Don't question, don't say anything—just remain calm and drive. Then, of course, there was the other thing: if there was something genuinely the matter with her, mentally, I would want to show her some courtesy, a bit of empathy. I made it a point to be this way on occasion.

We were all in the same boat, I reasoned. Some people can't take the pressure of life and crack. It happens. And the rest of us, who are able to hang on, ought to have the sense and responsibility to show some kindness. Of course, there was always that chance that you were being taken for a ride, used, taken advantage of.

I turn right on Pico. Take it slowly west toward Motor.

"You still want me to turn right on Motor?"

"Turn left here," she said, not shouting this time. We head south on Motor, through Cheviot Hills. She's eating chocolate chip cookies. Hands me one. I don't want it, but take it just the same.

"Eat it. They're good cookies."

I jam it in the ashtray.

"Turn left here," she says, when we reach Manning. We get on the Santa Monica Freeway, take it east, off at Crenshaw. South Central. To make it short, we arrive at her address. I take her stuff out, but she hasn't got money to pay me.

"This isn't right," I tell her. "I'm here trying to make a living. This isn't right. I've got twenty-two bucks on the meter."

"I know it ain't right. I'll pay you. It's my boyfriend who's got the money. He lives just five houses from here. Why don't you come on over with me?"

I close my trunk. Notice salt and cookie crumbs on my backseat. Exasperated is how I feel, as I pull away.

"Have it your way, motherfucker!" she's still shouting. "Don't you want your money? Fuck it!"

I'm glad to have her out of my cab. I make it back to the hotel. The tall bellhop wants nothing to do with it, doesn't want to hear it as I try to explain that I got burned.

"She wouldn't pay me," I tell him.

"I got nothing to do with that," he says, walking away. "Go inside, talk to the guys who put her in your cab."

I go in, to no avail. "We didn't know she couldn't pay you. I swear it," the skinny one explains. Bullshit, I say to that. Frustrated by it all: not getting paid, the time lost, the gas, all of it—the three hours I spent on the stand waiting for the fare. . . . What to do? Get more upset, or go back to the stand and try again?

The other drivers hear the story and think it's funny. Just like the Monday morning quarterback, everybody has the answer.

"Should have dumped her right there; asked for the money up front."

"You think that's always easy?"

I try to forget, but for the time being, I can't. What right did people like my fare have to mistreat others? The hotel is totally responsible. It was their fault. They knew what they were doing and exactly.

I return to the Tower, ask to speak to the manager. From the desk clerk I find out that the woman had owed them six hundred, had destroyed furniture in her room.

"So how could you people put somebody like that in my cab? Knowing she didn't have money to pay me?"

He goes in the back. Several minutes later a woman in her thirties appears. I give her my story. All she can do is apologize and say: "We aren't responsible for that."

"You put her in my cab knowing full well she couldn't pay me. She didn't pay for her room, right?"

"She paid for her room."

Now they're changing their story.

"You kept her car, isn't that right?"

"That's another story; but yes, we did keep her car."

She tells me to write my name and phone number down. "I can't promise you anything."

Where was the justice? Now, twenty-two bucks is not a lot of money (well, it's enough to a cabbie)—but it is also the principle of the thing. It just was not right. I work hard for my money. In fact, had pulled sixty-five hours without sleep just to keep my head above water—and then people do something like this.

You bet it angered me.

Then one of the bellhops gestures, says: "There; that's her boyfriend. Talk to him."

I go outside, explain the situation to the "boyfriend." He seems like a reasonable guy. Pleasant.

"She's got problems," he tells me. "She's on Lithium. I'm really not her boyfriend, just a friend."

"How do I get paid? Can you pay me?"

"I don't have money on me. I had to borrow money to take the bus up here."

"Well, what do I do? Can you help me out?"

"What can I tell you, man?" he says. "It ain't like she don't have any money—she just won a settlement, got ten grand—so that ain't it."

"You couldn't pay me, and then get it from her later?"

"I ain't got it on me, brother. If you want, you can give me your phone number and I'll see what I can do."

"Why don't you give me *your* number?"

He's not keen on the idea. I write down my number, for what good it is going to do. Thank the guy. He's still apologizing as I'm driving away. I had twenty-two bucks on the meter. And got a stale cookie for it instead.

I'm back on the stand at the Century Plaza. And Howie Lipowitz already knows the story. Picture Howie: loud, punch drunk, yellowish/silver crew cut pushing sixty with a face scarred and smashed in like a train wreck; and oh yeah, a former con with a red kerchief always dangling from the left rear pocket of his jeans. Macho Man Howie, who evidently took dick up the hind end (and let that scarf dangle proudly announcing the fact). One other thing, he carried a fully loaded Smith & Wesson .38 right in front, between the seats, for all to see.

Lipowitz often worked late into the night, and would doze off on the cab stand. Couple of months ago, early early one quiet, slow morning, the doorman blows his whistle, waking Howie. Howie, not quite alert, jumps in his seat, kicks the accelerator and keeps going at such a high rate of speed that he rams the front end of his cab into the lobby entrance. He walked away without a scratch that time, but had left a good section of the wall with a crack six feet in length from the ground up. He was lucky that they let him work the hotel. Now he was the one with the advice. The way it usually worked in life. The biggest fuck-ups are the ones with all the answers. I let him have his say; he was enjoying himself way too much for me to want to stop him. In addition to the above, Howie had been the guy giving me a hard time because I'd turned down four drunks about a week back.

"So you still think I shouldn't turn down drunks, Howie?"

He's laughing. "I heard," he says. "Should have done what I did." He'd had a drunk get in his cab the night before, took him for six bucks worth, and then the guy tells him: "I don't want to pay you. That's it. If you don't like it, too bad."

Now, Howie, being the certified screwball that he is, and by that I mean, the crazy fuck once, to prove that his .38 was loaded, as I sat in his backseat, he in front, on the Constellation side of the Plaza one day, held the goddamn gun in his hand, turned with it, holding it point-blank this way in front of my face—to *convince* me that the goddamn piece was loaded. The gun so close to my face I could see the bullets inside the chambers. That was the last time I sat in the 8-ball's cab to have a chat with him about anything. And the fucker was licensed to carry the .38. It's a nutty world. *Licensed; he was licensed.*

To get back to his tale and his drunk: Howie took it in stride. Instead of getting riled, he kept his cool, said to his fare (knowing they were a mere two blocks from the cop station in Culver City), "Wait a second: Let me get you closer to your place. Get back in." His drunk climbs back in the backseat, says to Howie: "You're a pretty good guy after all." "I try," had been Howie's comeback, as he pulls up in front of the cop station, only the guy back there is so drunk he doesn't get it. Howie turns to him: "Listen, let me just go in there and make a quick phone call, and then I'll drop you off in front of your front door. How's that sound?"

"Goddamn, you're a good guy. You're all right."

"Yeah, I know it."

Howie goes in, and comes out with two cops. They handcuff the drunk, and take him inside, book him. And all Howie had had on his meter was six dollars and ten cents. I was out $22.30, not counting tip. Like I say, that was some expensive chocolate chip cookie—that I never wanted any part of.

Later on, I managed to turn things around, kept a positive head. Took an insect fanatic out to the arboretum where they were having some kind of show on bugs from all over the world. That trip netted me sixty bucks. The weekend turned out okay after all, in spite of the lady with the chocolate chip cookies.

So next time you get in my cab and are about to say: You must meet lots of interesting people. . . .

Cruising For Action
A Chance "Cash" Register Taxicab Trip

He climbs in the cab at 2:30 in the a.m. On a Sunday night, a quiet, dead Sunday night, a fat cat banker from Montana or some place like that, away on a "bit of business." The rest of the family didn't come with, as they never do.

The guy wants to know about "some action"; he's talking about finding a prostitute. This is the posh Beverly-Wilshire Hotel in Beverly Hills and it's a dead night around here and not a whore in sight. I mention Sunset Strip. "That's where they hang out," I say, even though I got my doubts. It's a corpse of a night. If he wants to ride around looking for action, I'm game, as long as the meter's ticking.

"Aw-right," he says. "Let's go to Sunset."

I drop the flag, and we're off and running. Up Doheny, a right on Sunset, and we cruise.

A mile later we spot a boney-looking, *bow-legged* black chick who is so homely I almost don't say anything, but then do: "*There's one.*"

The guy looks and looks hard. Doesn't say a word.

We roll on.

Past closed restaurants, men's shops, a strip joint, disco, the director's guild—and happen on another "working girl," except this working girl is more *horrible looking* than the first, if that's possible.

I slow down at the curb. The nightmare walks up to the cab. I wait for a yea or nay from the well-fed porker in the backseat.

Finally he says: "Let's go get the other one."

I pull away. The nightmare flips us off, calls us *"Honky Shit Bastards!"*

We reach the bow-legged chick.

She's in the cab talking money.

"How much?" the beer belly says.

"How much can you spend?" the hooker counters, as they always answer that question that way. *"What chu got to spend, baby?"*

It's agreed on forty for head, and bowlegs insists I pull over behind the gas station so she can "do him" right away. I refuse. She keeps trying to talk me into letting her blow the guy in the backseat.

"No way," I tell her, and drive the three of us to the Beverly-Wilshire.

The banker (or whatever he did for a living) pays me; jumps out. Hurries inside the deserted hotel lobby. She follows quickly after him. And it's impossible for me not to start chuckling and shaking my head as I watch the heavy guy trying to keep a good distance ahead of the homely bowlegs and the bowlegs hurrying to catch up so as not to lose him and the big belly increasing his pace. It was funny as hell and I had to laugh. The big guy was desperate for action and yet just as desperate to put distance between himself and the common street whore so that he would not be seen with her by any of the night crew working the front desk.

As I slowly pull away, am still chuckling and shaking my head. Can't be helped. What a man won't go through to get his nuts off.

From the Grave

A Mini Nightmare

The corpse wanted me to join him. Ty Southfield was thirty-four when he slit his wrists, died in a bed soaked with his blood in a Burbank apartment across the street from the stables. The body had been discovered two days later by Chubby Elston, a guy he palled around with. I didn't know Ty very well, had seen him once or twice; he had appeared as an extra in a student film I made in the early 70s: he had allowed the use of his fishing boat for a scene, and he had appeared in another short film a mutual friend, Angus Gladwyn, had put together.

Ty seemed an easygoing sort, somewhat shy, balding, a bit on the portly side. Came from a family in Ohio that was, by no means, poor, I was to learn later from Elston.

Ty had been working as a dishwasher in a greasy spoon in the Valley when he took his life. He had ten grand in the bank and not many could really understand why he'd ended it. Ty had no social life, none to speak of, drove a junk heap of a car, slashed his wrists at thirty-four.

I think I had X-ray vision, or it just seemed that way in the dream. Ty's arms were outstretched in his grave. He kept motioning for me to join him. I think I kept asking "Why?" and he kept waving for me to just do it. *"Come on, it's all right down here."*

"Why, Ty?"

He kept smiling. "It's not as bad as everybody thinks. It's great. Peaceful. No hassles. I like it. You'll like it, too. You'll like it just fine."

"Ty, *I don't understand.*"

"Come on, join me."

The picture changed, and I saw President Reagan giving a speech on pornography and it was odd; he was trying to warn the audience to keep away from those sex ads in the skin mags, in particular ads promoting inflatable dolls. "Don't fool with that stuff," he advised. "You'll get ripped off."

"What?"

"You'll get ripped off. You'll never get your money's worth. Believe me; studies have been made. Don't waste your money—"

And while Reagan was making with the speech, I could hear Ty's voice coming in loud and clear, to Reagan's dismay: "Come on, Chance; I know you're miserable out there. I like you. I want to help."

I kept shaking my head at the image that had superimposed itself over Reagan's face, that image of Ty's arms fervently beckoning me from the coffin and I didn't know how much longer I could resist the temptation.

"I need time, Ty—I need time. . . . Things may change. . . . I'm only thirty—"

The phone rang, waking me. It was Angus.

"Chubby's girlfriend is having a surprise party for him Saturday. Can you make it?"

"What?"

"Chubby's girlfriend is throwing a surprise party for Chubby this

Saturday—and she's trying to get some of his friends together. I told her I'd see what I could do. Red can't make it. Jingo's going. Can you be there?"

"I don't know. . . . I work Saturday. . . ."

"I thought you were off Saturday. . . . What should I tell her?"

"I don't think she ought to call Ty. . . ." My head was spinning; I was in and out of the weird dream. Flashes of Ty Southfield waving his arms from the grave played with my psyche.

"Ty who?" Angus asked. (Ty had died five years ago.)

"Southfield," I said. A long pause followed, then Angus Gladwyn said: "Why did you say that?"

"I don't know," said I.

Death In The Fast Lane

He stared blankly at the notice that had arrived in the mail two days ago. The notice said to either pay rent within eight days or vacate the premises. Floyd Dangler turned out the light, sat in the one chair in his room and pulled on his beer. It was only 5:30 p.m., but it was already dark outside. The traffic on Wilshire, less than a block away, was buzzing strong with the rush hour.

Floyd thought about the particular words they had used in the letter: NOTICE TO PAY RENT OR QUIT (within date stated). *Pay up, or else you're out in the street.* He contemplated writing them a letter and telling them what cruel, unfeeling leeches they were. They didn't give a damn about people, they didn't care. The owners of the building, two brothers out of Beverly Hills, were millionaires, owned apartment buildings and commercial real estate, were practicing attorneys themselves and were constantly making more money and every time they came around to collect the rents from the manager would pull up with their fat wives in brand new Mercedes Benzes. They never did anything for the tenants or to improve the building and were jacking up the rent at every opportunity.

Floyd had lived here two years now. And during the first year and a half he had never been late with the rent once. He had first worked as a dishwasher, and moved on to waiting tables, while trying to get work as an actor. He wasn't having much luck with the casting directors, but he had managed to pay his rent on time.

He stared in the dark, pulled on the bottle.

What was happening to the world? Nobody gave a damn about anybody. There was only one thing on everyone's mind: money; money and more money. The rich weren't satisfied with just being rich, they had to get richer—and the poor suffered and suffered, toiled at their jobs that hardly paid a livable wage, toiled. But times were tough. The "New Administration" had begun making incredible cuts, cuts that affected a lot of people, a lot of hard-working citizens. People had quit going out, to movies, eateries, night clubs—and Floyd had been laid off from three different places in less than five months. He had been trying to find work for nearly a month now, and had no luck. The kind of work he was qualified to do wasn't available. He had a couple of years of college, but that made little difference. He had hit bottom and he knew it. This was it, Floyd concluded. The end of the line, man. Nowhere to go, brother. Thirty-five years old and a certified loser. Now he certainly knew what the phrase meant: *born loser.* That's what I am, a born loser. For sure. I know it, I know it.

He emptied the bottle, reached inside the refrigerator and got another. He lingered a moment before closing the door. There were four bottles left. Four beers, a rotten tomato, some stale cheese and a bottle of *A1 Steak Sauce* he had bought ages ago.

He uncapped the beer bottle. Poured brew down his throat. A siren wailed past (one of many). Nothing unusual for the neighborhood that housed so many elderly people, the dead and dying.

Someday, maybe soon, real soon, they would be taking him away like that; that would be his exit—in a screaming ambulance.

There was only one person he could blame, not that he had the energy anymore, that he wanted to or would even consider it, only one: himself. Eleven years of toiling away in a sewer called LA, eleven years of struggle and more struggle, pursuing a dream that would never happen, that never could happen, not for him—for others, yes, maybe—but not for Floyd Dangler. Not Floyd Dangler. Of the handful who did make it there were hundreds, thousands like Floyd Dangler who didn't, who ended up insane, suicidal or dead, worthless. I'm no good anymore, he thought. Washed up, used up, burned out. I'm breathing, breathing, but that's all.

He was a veteran, true, he'd been to 'Nam——but that hardly had anything to do with it. It had been over a decade ago. He'd gotten through it, made it. It was all the rest of the bullshit that finally chipped away at your sanity, the rejections, the living in tiny rooms, the no car, the insecurity, insomnia. No decent woman would ever want anything to do with someone like that—and he knew it. Did he ever. He had lived with a woman about three years back, had loved her, truly loved her; but it didn't work. Money problems, always money problems. In addition, Floyd had been depressed most of the time, complained about his career not going anywhere, always moody, on the edge—and he never realized how much damage this had done to the relationship until it was too late and the woman had wanted out, and Floyd became suicidal, but he got through it.

I got through it, he thought. I made it through that one. Dealt with the aftereffects of the war, fucked up childhood, the breakup. But I'm running out of steam, baby. No more steam. No gusto, no nothing. I was tough once, I had some guts once, but no more, no more, man. I'm only human, I'm only human. There's only so much a man can take, only so much, before he finally cracks, finally. . . . He felt a tear forming in his right eye and slowly descend down his cheek, down across his Adam's apple. He wiped it, the eye, took a strong pull. Ah, the Magic Elixir, the only comforter, the only . . . But it was also suicide juice. Beer always brought tears to his eyes, depressed him, but it was OK. This time it was OK. There was nowhere to go now, no place left.

All those years he had stayed away from the Boulevard, the depressing, nightmarish Hollywood Boulevard, and had only ventured up there on occasion to see a movie at the Chinese, or buy a book at Pickwick's. The prostitutes, the transvestites, the winos, pimps, junkies, that made the Boulevard their home, did a good job of keeping everyone else away. But tonight, he thought, tonight he would officially become one of them. No more false hopes, no more dreaming, no more pretending he was better, above it, no more. Tonight he would join the scum. He would join them.

He downed the rest of the contents in the bottle, got into the old overcoat, stuffed the remaining bottles of beer in his pockets, put his dark shades on, and walked outside. Paranoia hit him the second the front door closed behind him. *Paranoia,* that meanest mother of them all, *paranoia.* But it would be OK, it would be fine—he'd be with his fellow losers soon enough; yeah, he'd be with them, walking around, staring off into space. He would join up with the zombies.

He walked north on Hauser, through the dimly lit section of Park LaBrea where a security car tailed him until he reached Third Street. At Third Floyd stayed on Martel, continued north, avoiding the wider, better traveled streets.

Yeah, he thought, nobody knew anything about compassion, kindness, all those things that mattered, all those things he himself had become a stranger to, all those fine little things his mother had tried to instill in him when he was a kid (the times she wasn't behaving like a loon), the qualities one needed to be a decent human being: courtesy and generosity of spirit. . . . All that was gone, part of the past. Nobody was like that anymore; they didn't know how to be, or care to be. The world was a mess, a cesspool; degenerates everywhere you went: thieves, killers, prostitutes; users and more users. Dirt. There was so much dirt. God, what's become of us? What's happened? Weren't any of these people brought up by parents who cared? Who tried to teach them anything? What's happening to the human race?

A junk heap of a car pulled up alongside him. The bearded filthy-looking creep in it whistled at Floyd and kept whistling. Floyd stopped, looked at him.

The man kept smiling. Stopped the car.

"I give a great blow job," the man said. "The best."

Floyd stared at the car for a silent moment, then slowly walked toward it.

"You interested?" the man asked.

Floyd continued toward the car without uttering a word.

For some reason the smile dropped from the man's face. "Some other time," he said. And the junk heap drove away. Floyd stood there in the street a while, got back on the sidewalk, and continued north.

At the corner of Selma, two male hustlers in skintight white jeans were sharing a joint. Floyd stopped, pulled on his bottle, and watched the faggots. They had their arms around each other, as they smoked the joint. The scene was only making him sicker. He drank his beer and watched. Pretty soon a Mercedes pulled up with a guy in a suit and tie. The faggots, after exchanging some words with the driver, got in the car. The car drove away. The junk heap drove past again. The beard didn't look at him once.

Floyd finished off the beer, and stuck the empty bottle back in his pocket. He walked to the Boulevard. They were there, in filthy clothes, spent, rummies young and old. Some were even on skates. One black guy was in green tights, and had a harmonica in his mouth, as he rolled past Floyd.

"You're hopeless, muthafuckah!" the guy shouted at Floyd and continued on.

The sick cursing out the sick, Floyd thought. Yep, it's a hopeless goddamn world we're living in, he thought. Yep.

He walked east a while, stopped in front of the magic shop, and the teddy bear was still in the window, that teddy bear his girl had expressed interest in while they were still together. He was aware of her twenty-sixth birthday coming up, thought what a perfect gift it would still be for her, a fun gift; but as usual, you couldn't afford anything like that—so forget it. The teddy bear stood a good five feet and cost fifty-five bucks.

Two Mexicans in army jackets stopped long enough to ask him for some money. When Floyd told them he didn't have any, the greasier and more pimply of the two said: "All we find, we keep?" and were about to search him. Floyd had taken a step back, and said: "Go ahead."

There had been a cop car across the street, and the Mexicans had continued on. Floyd had spit on the ground and made it to the all-night newsstand on Wilcox. He had been a good hour and a half in there going through the girlie magazines when the clerk had told him that it just wasn't right. "You're looking at the magazines and not buying anything. You'll have to either make a purchase or leave." Floyd had stared at the man for a moment and walked out and walked to Sunset.

There were some black hookers lingering, working the streets. Floyd approached one of them. The hooker gave him a quick once over and told him to get the fuck away from her.

"You hear, mothafuckah? I'll get my old man after yo ass!"

"What're you afraid of?" Floyd asked. "Huh? What're you afraid of?"

"Fuck off, hear? *Fuck off!*"

Floyd walked, ended up back on the same corner where he'd seen the two male hustlers in the white pants. There was a church there on the corner. Floyd contemplated urinating in the doorway. Just as he was about to unzip his fly, a gray Corvette pulled up to the curb, the door on the passenger side opened, and a male rolled out of it and into the gutter. The Corvette sped away.

Floyd Dangler stood there, watching, as the guy staggered to his feet, clutching his stomach, moaning; tears and snot and blood streaming from his eyes and mouth. The guy was probably in his late teens or early twenties, and staggered against the steps to the church.

"God, I'm hurt," he cried. "I'm hurt. Help me. . . . Jesus, help me. . . ."

Floyd's jaw got tight, the sight and the whimpering was making him sick, so damn sick. He walked to the kid on the steps. The top part of the kid's jeans in the fly area was torn, the two breast pockets of his Hawaiian shirt; the buttons missing. Blood oozed from his busted jaw, and there was the unmistakable stench of excreta in the air that only added to Floyd's nausea.

The kid glanced up. "Help me, please help me. . . ."

Floyd leaned over, got his arms around the kid's chest and dragged him to a darker, more secluded area, the whole time trying not to breathe, fighting to keep from throwing up. As he lowered the kid down on the ground, a stream of yellowish/gray liquid shot out of the kid's mouth. Puke.

Floyd stood back, watched, motionless, the fingers wrapped tightly around the neck of the bottle inside his overcoat pocket. He took the bottle out, cracked the lower half against the curb, then drew the bottleneck slowly toward the male hustler's face. It took the kid a moment to realize what was happening, but by then it was too late to even make a plea. The jagged edge of the bottleneck in Floyd's hand dug deep into the kid's throat repeatedly and one final move that sliced the neck open just under the Adam's apple.

Floyd remained at a crouch and watched as the punk gasped and the blood spurted. After a moment, Floyd Dangler stood up and walked north on Highland, north toward the freeway. He reached the base of the south-bound Hollywood Freeway on-ramp, got out of his clothes, folding each item carefully and placing it on the ground at his feet: overcoat, shirt, pants, socks, boxers. The shoes? The shoes he placed on top of this neat little pile that summed up his life and existence, what he was worth.

He urinated standing up, then squatted to defecate. When he was done, he rose and slowly walked up the on-ramp to the freeway. He entered the slow lane without ever turning his head to see what was coming up from behind. There were cars, traffic—whether it was in his lane or not did not matter. He heard a vehicle of some type honk its horn, then tires screech and swerve off to someplace.

He did not bother turning his head, no; the goal was to keep walking, make gradual progress to his left, and eventually all the way to the far left and what awaited him there: at long last, a taste of the fast lane.

The Hard Bitch

Starring PI Choo-Choo Buschitski
in a Long Short Story

This case I had done, for the most part, for the cash. I was still behind on the office rent. It didn't worry me all that much. I'd been here a long time and the owner was reasonable. But what did bother me were the heartless Santa Anas that whipped at you so fast and hard it made your eyes water.

It was after 2:00 a.m. and I'd been tailing the fathead from bar to sleazy bar since 9:00 p.m. I needed to take a shit and I was cold. My feet ached. I was horny, too, as I usually am, but pussy was about the last thing on my mind.

I wrapped the trench coat tightly about me and crossed Santa Monica Boulevard, waited for the douchebag to cross Western, and followed. The guy was in a gray suit, black overcoat, chunky and bald-headed. His face was red; in fact, his whole skull had a red glow to it. The booze, I guess. He staggered up to the porno theatre, paid his five bucks at the window and went in. I waited a second and did the same.

I opened a door on my right, waited for my eyes to adjust and started looking for the guy and couldn't find him. I turned and returned to the lobby. He was coming out of the men's room with a wad of toilet paper sticking out of his overcoat pocket. I guess he was going to beat his meat. I went in the john, got some TP (just in case I felt like doing the same). You never could tell, sometimes these pornos could get you really worked up. Usually, these things left me feeling like shit, depleted and sick, because the scumbags on the screen looked so pathetic and used up.

My man selected a seat on the far right side all by himself. I sat in the middle. I knew the porno wouldn't do it for me this time. They had dog shit on the screen. I used the tissue to blow my nose with. I looked to my right: the fat man was beating his pud under his overcoat. When he was through, he got up and walked out of the theatre.

Shit, just when I was starting to get warm.

He walked to Hollywood Boulevard and then continued east for about three or four blocks to where his car sat. He got in his Cadillac, a much later model and year than mine. I got in my Fleetwood.

I tailed him to Western, up to Franklin, then west for three blocks. He made a left turn and parked. I waited in my car and didn't get out until he was inside one of those two-story buildings. Then I had to run to make sure I didn't lose the cocksucker. *But I had.* I knew he was in the building, but had no idea what apartment. The lights were on in half the units. The tenants were asleep but the light had been left on to ward off burglars. A tv blared from somewhere. I checked out the first floor, climbed the wooden staircase to the second floor balcony and walked slowly. A couple could easily be heard fucking in the first apartment. I moved on. Nothing in the second. Another tv (or radio. . .). I walked. That's when the fat fuck appeared coming out of the third apartment with a blond in a sheer negligee, arms wrapped around his fat neck. She was clutching some bills in one of her hands.

She was smiling and gave him a big smacking kiss before he left. I pretended to be fumbling with some keys at the other end of the balcony.

When the fat man was gone, I rapped on the blond's door. She opened it, expecting it to be the fat man. She looked at me, wondered if I were a cop. I held up a business card. She shrugged.

"I was hired by the fat guy's wife," I told her. It was enough to register a degree of concern on that vicious, although pretty enough face.

"I'm freezing my ass off out here," I said.

"What do you want?"

"Well," I said, "if Fatty Arbuckle's old lady finds out he's got a sweet young thing like you on the side, there goes your sugar daddy. Need I say more?"

She stood there.

"Let me the fuck in." And I pushed her aside and walked in.

"Just what the hell do you think you're doing?"

"I gotta use your john. I haven't shit in days."

"In there," she motioned. I rushed in, dropped my trousers and dropped a pile and a load off my shoulders. The bathroom was nice and neat and smelled like a rose garden. Lots of pretty figurines and perfume bottles, shampoo bottles, lotions and skin creams. There was a dildo on the floor, a magazine on bondage. I picked up the magazine, leafed through it. The photos were in black & white, pictures of women tied and gagged and being either whipped or fucked by naked studs wearing black leather masks. There were photos of interracial couples.

Not that I was ever into pain when it came to romance, but looking at all that pussy got me pretty hard. I wiped my ass and kept looking. The blond walked in. She was calm, in control, smoking a cigarette.

"That kind of shit turn you on?" she asked.

"Not really," I said. "Does watching a man take a shit *turn you on?*"

She blew smoke. "Sometimes," she said.

I got my hands around my cock and just held it like that. She was watching and she was smiling. I got a really good look at her for the first time. She was in heels, pink heels, and the negligee was pink as well. The patch between her upper thighs was dark and there was plenty there. Big strong hips as were her legs. A slim waist. She had large tits, maybe 38, 39.

"What does a guy like that pay you?" I asked.

She blew some more smoke. "Couple of grand a month," she said. "Never touches me. Just likes to watch while I masturbate, or likes me to watch while he rubs his pathetic little dick. Sometimes he creams in my face. Usually, mostly though, I just listen to his tales of woe. Easy money, wouldn't you say?"

I didn't answer, and stroked my meat.

"What've you got there? How much?"

I shrugged. "I don't know. Eight or nine. Haven't measured lately."

She chuckled at that. "Bullshit. I know the way men are, measuring that fucking thing every chance you get."

She had me chuckling as well.

"Is that what the fat guy does?"

She was nodding her head. "He's got four inches. Always measuring to see if it's getting any bigger. Even had me buying some of those creams and phony gizmos to make it grow. Never has, of course. I'm not complaining. Two grand a month is a nice piece of change."

"Why don't you turn around and bend over?" I said. "I want to kiss your ass."

She did as I asked. "I want you to cum in my mouth," she said. "Okay?"

"Yeah. Fine."

I kissed her butt, got my tongue under and licked her pussy. She turned and stood up and had her cunt pressed against my face. I kept licking a while longer. She dropped to her knees and started sucking. I took the cigarette from her and dropped it in the sink. I had my head back against the wall. She knew exactly what she was doing. A high-class bitch who fucked and sucked for the big bucks. She worked it and worked it, like she was really enjoying it. I had my hands clamped around the back of her head, forced my cock in her mouth ever deeper and shot juice. There was a lot there, almost two whole days' worth and she damn near gagged on it. I screamed and held on. *Goddamn.*

It took me a while to recover. I flushed the toilet, got up.

"How about a drink?" she offered. I asked for some hot coffee or tea instead. She showed me around the apartment: a large bedroom with a fancy brass bed (of course), pink sheets, all silk, a variety of sexy gowns and negligees. There was an aquarium in the living room, a color set, stereo. Tidy and comfortable.

After my tea arrived, she said: "So . . . are you going to blow the two grand a month for me?"

"I haven't decided."

"I wouldn't charge you," she said, "if you wanted to keep seeing me."

"I'd like to fuck you about a dozen times or so—then I'd have to decide."

"Would she have to know? The guy's wife, I mean."

"It's a matter of principle. I like pussy and all that. I gave the woman my word I'd do my best. I try to do a good job. Why don't we discuss it in about a week from now?"

"Whatever you like."

She had gone in the bathroom, applied some knockout, instant erection perfume and returned. My cock was rigid again. I didn't know when she'd had the chance to make the phone call, but somehow she did, maybe she had a phone in the john that I hadn't noticed, because two goons in dark suits had stepped through the front door and they weren't selling *Trojans.* One was lugging a ball bat, the other a gun. The bitch stood there, arms akimbo, a smug expression on her perfect face.

"Shit," I sighed.

"What's your story, Mack?" the one with the gun said.

"Simple really," I said. "Had to take a dump bad—and this young lady was pleasant and courteous enough to allow me the use of her toilet."

"Cut the bullshit!" the woman snapped. "We stand to lose the fat boy's bucks if this asshole talks. Vince, we gotta do something."

Vince, the one with the piece, lit a cigarette, all done expertly, movie style, with one hand. The hair was dark and slicked back, a la George Raft. He had rings on both hands, a bracelet, so did the other guy. Shirts open down to the hairy chest. Gold pendants dangling, gleaming.

"What's your racket, Mack?" Vince said.

"He's some sleazy private dick," the blond said. Since she was doing all my answering for me, I remained quiet and contemplated taking Dutch Shultz & Co., and wondered if I really could. They had the advantage, so far.

"Celia?" Vince said calmly, cooly. "Shut your sweet lips for a fuckin' second here, will you?"

She fired up a fresh cigarette.

"I want to hear it straight, Mack," he said to me. He was blowing smoke rings, just like the blond had done earlier, only better. His were really perfect. I almost commented on it.

"Like the lady says, I'm a private peeper."

"So the fuck you doin' here?"

"Like she says: I tailed the Pillsbury dough boy over, had to use the crapper. About it. I may or may not report it to his concerned spouse. Nothing really complicated, as you can well see."

"You gonna spill the beans about the fat turd having a bitch on the side? 'Cause if you do, man—shit, it's a lot of fuckin' jack you gonna blow for us. Fats really digs Celia here. Been seein' her for over six months now."

He blew some more smoke across the room. "Who knows, it may go on indefinitely." That last one had been an effort for him. I sighed.

"Like I told your little gal here: I'll know in about a week—"

"How do you mean?"

"He says he wants to fuck me for a week before he decides," the blond said.

The goons chuckled.

"Can you blame me?" I said. "She's a shag and a half."

They continued chuckling. Vince put the heat away. I got up, walked to the door.

"I'll tell you one thing, private dick," Vince said to me, "we lose that fat turd's cash, it's on your head. We take it out of your fucking hide."

I don't know; that irked me, just a touch. Two-bit punks telling me they had the world by the balls, when in fact they didn't have so much as a pubic hair, not as far as I was concerned.

I sent a kick into bat boy's nuts, and continued with my pivot in a flowing motion that sent a hard and near fatal blow into Vince's face. Bone crunched. Both were down and groggy. I picked up Vince's piece, emptied the contents into my left pocket.

"Now what're you gonna do, Valentino? Huh?" He was busy checking to see if his nose was busted. A good guess said it was—in more than one place.

"When you start telling people what to do . . . make sure their name isn't Felix 'Choo-Choo' Buschitski. Make sure they're normal, everyday slobs who comprehend fear and pain."

He kept fucking with his nose. The other one was gritting his teeth. I think the kick may have cancelled his love life for at least a week, or maybe for good.

I looked up at Celia, who just stood there not knowing what to do, dumbfounded and nearly scared. But she was a tough bitch who'd been around and seen plenty.

"What now?" she said.

"I'm a nasty motherfucker," I said, "but I never hurt a man who didn't try some shit on me first—and I never fucked a woman who didn't want it as much as I did, or seemed to anyway."

"You saying I still got to fuck you for a week?"

"No, you don't have to do jack."

"I don't want to lose that easy money."

I rose to my feet. "Do as you like," were my parting words, and I was back in the windy night.

Experience, the best teacher in the world, and that teacher was telling me as I started the Caddy up that at least one of the two cheap hoods would be coming back for a little payback—maybe with a little extra muscle next time and maybe not right away. Vinnie didn't strike me as a quitter, not when there was this much jack at stake. That meant more problems, and it also meant I would have to raise Roxanne Gloogal's retainer.

I returned to my apartment near Third and Alvarado and slept for twelve hours. I had a beer for breakfast and took a walk down Alvarado to the office. The sleazy masseuses made their pitch. I felt hungover and didn't say a word.

I climbed the steps, turned on the Ansaphone. Roxanne Gloogal, Arbuckle's wife wanted me to call her. The other message was from a midget actor I'd done some work for before. He wanted his six-foot-two wife found again. Bullshit to that. I never liked repeaters. Once they're out of my life, I want them to stay out. A job done once is enough. That's it. I knew one thing: I wasn't in a great mood. I hated being this way. The third message was from Vince. I easily recognized the voice. "*You're a dead duck.*" Click.

That was it.

I reached for a beer, then it started to come up. Maybe too much sleep or not the right food or because no food, or the tea from the night before, the smell of pesticide and urine—I ran down the hallway and into the john and puked for about twenty minutes. I felt better. Rinsed out my mouth with water and returned to the office.

Celia was there, alone. She looked better than the night before, better than any model *Cosmo* ever used. A white tight dress that accentuated all the curves. I don't think I had it in me to shag right away, but I had a boner. She sat down in my chair, propped her legs up on the desk. She was smiling. Well, I don't know. Some hookers got a piece, a small portion in their hearts that's still human. I say some, because most are just hard, the ones I've seen. It's not difficult to understand. Celia, on the other hand, was a bitch through and through. A cunt, a man-hating cunt who would get everything she could out of them, any way she could. Perhaps deep down she was a dyke. None of that made any difference to me. I would fuck her again probably, operate the same way she operated. Bang 'em and forget 'em.

My cock stayed hard.

"What do you think?" she said.

I lifted my beer.

She was lighting a cigarette, as always, the way her kind thinks it is cool to do. I felt like smacking her across the face.

"What do I think?"

"Yes, Choo-Choo. What do you think?"

"You are *one hundred percent genuine cunt.* No ands, ifs, or buts. Shit through and through."

She kept smoking her cigarette, but the smile was gone.

"And who the fuck are you, may I ask? A degencrate Peeping Tom, spying on the helpless and confused, who makes a living snitching on them, ruining their lives. What I do may be low, honey—but it helps that poor bastard to know someone like me. What's so fucking *noble* about what you do? *You make me sick.*" She was standing. "You got me to suck you off because you knew I couldn't turn you down. I couldn't. You had me."

"Bullshit," I said, without raising my voice. "Bullshit to that. Nobody made you do jack. You lapped it up, '*honey,*' 'cause you crave it. But you're a bitch, see? And I know it—and you can't stand it that someone can see right through you. Your looks don't mean shit to me other than that I get wood. After fucking someone like you, that's it, it's over. I use cunts like you, and forget about it. I know how to deal with dog shit like you and it burns you up. You can't stand it. And you know something? I love it. I love it, baby." I was chuckling, and pulled on my beer.

"You're a creep." She indicated the mess outside: multi-colored junkers and the losers in them that the street traffic consisted of and their next-of-kin on foot on the sidewalks: transients, professional panhandlers, drunks, junkies, dealers, no-class street whores and out of work low-wage earners who couldn't hold down a job long enough to get their hands on one of those pathetic heaps. "You're like all that shit out there. You're part of this fucking sewer, that's why you like it so much. You and that asshole across the hallway: what's his name? *Doc Holiday* and that *skirt-chasing alkie creep Woody Putsky.* Make me ill."

I sat in my chair. "Leave any time," I said. The beer was fine. "Guys like Gloogal are like putty in your hands. You say jump, they say how high? You say roll over, play dead—they do it all. Guys like me know how to get to a broad like you. I know your weakness. I make the rules. You either play along, or you don't play, period. I call the shots."

"So what the hell is it you want?"

"From you? Nothing."

She was smiling again. Trying to bring back the cool.

"See," I said, "with a bitch like you I either get it or don't get it. If I get it, fine—if not, I beat off. Simple as that. Like right now, for instance. I'm hard. We can either do the nasty, or I just do this." I took my meat out and started stroking. I got the lube out and rubbed it over the length of my prick.

"So what does that prove?"

"It proves you've got the intelligence of an average mutt. It proves I like to masturbate—especially in front of a hot cunt like you."

"I want to fuck you," she said.

"I want you out of here," I told her. "You're probably a lousy lay. You give OK head. I doubt you're good at anything else. Like most of your type: all looks. Just looks. Show. I've been to bed with a few."

She reached for the zipper down at the bottom of her dress, pulled it up, all the way up to around her waist. And was about to take the dress off. I told her to leave it on. I liked it that way. She lifted the dress to about half her waist, revealing a hairy cunt and ass. No panties. She moved closer.

"You like it up the ass, bitch?"

"Not especially."

"I always like to fuck a cunt like you in the ass," I said. Got her to lean against the edge of the desk for support and slid it up her tight asshole. She had firm cheeks, large and round, the kind of ass that always drives me wild.

I pumped. She made sounds like it was hurting just a bit. Fuck that, I kept on.

"Rub your pussy," I told her. "Get your clit."

She did, and started moaning. I continued pumping. Withdrew it for a second, applied more baby oil, and got it back in there. My strokes were slow and easy and went all the way. I stayed with it for about ten minutes that way and shot juice. She came herself, or acted like it. I didn't care. I had gotten mine and it had been even better than the blow job she'd given me the night before. I slumped back in the swivel. She was wiping the sweat from my forehead. She even planted a couple of kisses on my nose and lips. She smelled like beauty, pure and heavenly, but I knew different. I opened my eyes. She was licking my forehead now, moved down toward my left ear, then the right.

I reached for two beers. Handed her one. She sat on a corner of the desk. "You really believe all that about me?" she wanted to know.

I pulled on my bottle.

"You really think I'm a bitch?'

Shit, I grinned. "Yep," I said. "And we both know it."

She was grinning as well.

"But it's okay, honey, you're not to blame, none of us is to blame, the way I see it. You're a victim—we're all victims, of circumstance, you know?"

She was pensive when she lit the cigarette. "I never looked at it that way," she said.

"What the hell," I added. "Nobody's perfect. What riles me is when people try to take me for a sucker. It really gets my goat."

"I guess I know what you mean," she said. "Like the way Vince tried to do."

I nodded. "And the way you tried to do." Maybe it was all so funny now, but it had taken a lot to strip away the phony bullshit and get at the truth, at some sort of truth. As one wonders what the truth really might be.

"I'd like to keep seeing you," she said. "And it's got nothing to do with Googles or Doodles, or whatever the fuck his name is."

I shrugged.

"It was great," I said, "but I have a tendency to get tired of routine fast—and balling the same woman falls into routine."

"Hmm, I never heard that one before—then again, can't say I've ever met anyone like you before, either." She pulled on her bottle. "You're actually suggesting you might get tired of fucking me?"

I sighed. "Yeah," I said.

"Do you know what that means?"

I just looked back at her.

"That means to me it's back to the analyst for another six months."

I laughed, for it dawned on me only then that Googles was a psychoanalyst. That was how she had gotten involved with him in the first place. She wanted to know what I was laughing about. I explained. She thought it was funny as well.

"He's suicidal," she said. "I know it's not funny, he turned to *me* for help. *I saved him—and not the other way around.*"

"It's not unusual," I said. "Most of your shrinks are nuts."

"I'm beginning to believe it."

"It's true."

She stubbed her cigarette out. "Wanna go again?"

I said I didn't feel like it right away. I had Vince on my mind, and then there was the decision to be made about Gloogal.

She got up, retouched her makeup. Shit, there was no mystery at all, I thought, looking at her. Dealing with women like her, or dealing with anybody. Truth. But getting to it was goddamn painful and debilitating at times, and even deadly.

"So what's Vince all about?" I asked.

She shrugged. "A pimp; out of Vegas, I guess. That's where I met him anyway. He's hung, good looks; he *had* good looks. We were shacked for a while. He got me johns. I got some, or most I should say, on my own. I got a condo in Vegas. Maybe you could visit sometime."

"What's his modus operandi?" I said. "How's he work?"

"He might bring in a new goon or two, fresh muscle—but that would be money he might not like to spend. A good, good nose job is gonna cost him plenty. And that other guy who was with him—I don't think he'd want to fool with you after what you did to him."

She said to call her sometime, and was gone.

I lied, if only slightly, about a bitch like her being easy to forget. Oh, it could be done—and always, it was the best thing to do. It took me a week to get her out of my mind. That's when Vince, with a different bat boy (as Celia had predicted), plus a third goon made their appearance. I had just been leaving the Gloogals' spread in Pasadena one evening (I spilled the beans on Gloogal. I don't think the wife wanted a divorce, merely a stop put to the cheating). A bullet hit me in the right calf and I went down, rolling in the wet grass and ending in the gutter where my Caddy was parked. I heard them talking. Vince was sure he had nailed me, but not sure I was dead just yet.

Some are born dumb and die dumb, and some, perhaps the same ones, got that stupid macho bullshit warping their common sense, because they somehow believe as true men, mean mothers that they are, things must and will go the way they like them to, because if they don't, they will and have the capacity and/or ability to kick ass. Vince and his fools were that confused and screwed up. And of course, that elbow to

Vince's head had undoubtedly jarred what little brains he had, because they were coming at me, spread out maybe, but coming to finish it off. I had my .38 out. I was bleeding and hurt, but it hadn't been the first time.

'Nam had toughened me up. One didn't die from most bullet wounds. One often died from the sheer shock of being hit. But fuck all that—a flesh wound didn't mean jack shit to me. I was losing blood and that I didn't like at all.

"He's armed probably," the dummy (Vince) said. "Watch it."

I got the .32 out of the rig on my ankle and tossed it out to where they could easily see it.

"Crawl out, motherfucker," Vince said. "Get out in the open."

"You got me, asshole," I told him. "I quit."

All three chuckled, especially Vince. I guess he really liked that.

"You busted my nose, motherfucker. It'll never be the same. Come out."

"You got me in the *huevos.* I can't move."

They came. I aimed and squeezed off a round. Vince's hands flew to his face as he dropped to the wet pavement. I squeezed off a couple more slugs and got the others. I limped over to check them out. Dead. All three. A job well done. Clean. The world had three less dirtbags to worry about.

I made it back to the Gloogals' residence, dialed the rollers. If they wanted to talk to me they could find me at the Hollywood Kaiser and that I needed some patching up. They came around just as the night duty doc was finishing up bandaging my leg. When all that was done, the cops promised me they had more questions and not to leave town. I was wheeled to my Caddy in a wheelchair by a friendly, if hefty, black lady in a white nurse's outfit. I drove over to Celia's. She was in tears when I got there, and I knew it had nothing to do with me, nor did it have anything to do with Gloogal (as he had left her a tidy sum for having been good to him). I didn't know what she was in tears about. She didn't offer to say, and I didn't ask. I suppose even a hard bitch like her has that tiny little spot way down in that heart of hers that is human, and not even all the hardness in the world can wipe it out completely.

* * *

LUSTMORD:
Anatomy of a Serial Butcher
Book One (of Two)

By KIRK ALEX

Blurb & Novel Excerpt

Who knew the minister next door
was also a sadistic predator?

Cecil Omar Biggs is not your average man of the cloth. By day, he appears to be a hardworking preacher, but once night descends upon the quiet Southern California neighborhood where Biggs resides, his darker self emerges. Living a double life as a sex fiend and brutal murderer, he enjoys luring innocent victims into his basement lair by any means possible.

Converting an old house into a church, Biggs becomes the perfect wolf in sheep's clothing, which also puts him in the ideal position to attract his unsuspecting prey. He lives to satisfy his sinister appetites without remorse or limits, indulging in his more violent tendencies as soon as the sun goes down by torturing and killing the women he abducts in his dungeon of doom.

But how long can Biggs keep up the nice-guy-next-door pretense while secretly living as a homicidal maniac? And what happens when the locals start suspecting that there's more to this seemingly harmless Bible-thumper than meets the eye?

A WORD OF CAUTION

**"And if you gaze for long into an abyss,
the abyss gazes also into you."
–Friedrich Nietzsche**

Translation: this one is not for the faint of heart, nor the weak of belly. Foretold is forewarned.

I started **LUSTMORD: Anatomy of a Serial Butcher** back in 1987, and it is January 17, 2013, as I write this. How many years is that? Twenty-six? Give or take. I say give or take because somewhere in there, during the mid 1990s, I had to lay off the thing for about five years. Why? Nightmares. Cold sweats. Unable to sleep. Why? Subject matter. Some of it was too damn horrific and the images wouldn't go away at the end of the day. Five years. Not to mention another three years when I could only face the book for about four or five months at a time. The shit was sick and depraved. Fucking brutal. I needed a break.

Why go anywhere near the subject matter, then? Why fool with it? Because I have to bounce around, move from genre to genre, or go batty—and because if I'm going to do a book about a sociopath, you better believe one thing: I am going to treat the material with absolute honesty. There is no other way. I did not want to whitewash (or sugarcoat) any of it, the way certain writers like to do, or the way some, rather, most Hollywood flicks treat the material: by having the unpleasant stuff happen off screen, or else it's done with gimmicks and cheesy effects. I wanted it raw, and I wanted it to be disturbing—because when it happens, the way it happens in real life, that's what it is: appalling, venal, sickening and twisted. So I repeat, read at your own risk.

The author/publisher is not responsible for any nervous breakdowns, facial tics, insomnia, depression, loss of appetite, loss of hair, sexual dysfunction, bouts of insanity, marriages and/or relationships disintegrating, time spent in therapy, stays in the bughouse, shakes, quakes, headaches, heart problems, vomiting, nausea, episodes of anxiety, suicidal tendencies or a sudden, inexplicable urge to do bodily harm to your fellow humans, and any other ailments, be they large or small, that you may experience as a result of having read **LUSTMORD: Anatomy of a Serial Butcher.** You have been thoroughly advised. Proceed at your own peril.

K. A.

CHAPTER 1

They were into it. Heard more than he wanted to.

"J.J., don't!"

"Shut your mouth, whore!"

"I'll be good! I promise, J.J.!"

"I told you to shut your hole!"

"Don't hit me, J.J. You better not hit me no more!"

"I'll beat you to death! Filthy heifer cunt!" Slaps and screams followed. "Why, you ain't even a good whore! Where's my whiskey money, bitch? Spent on shoes and ice cream for that worthless little shit? Why come? Since when are the little bastard's wants more important than mine?"

More slaps followed, screaming. The next sound was the male's, a deep grunt, as though on the receiving end himself. Furniture was thrown, dishes. The woman shrieked.

"We're out of ass-wipe, heifer, and you got nerve to waste money on ice cream and shoes for the little pissy!" Dogs barked; a real ruckus was in progress up there. The boy pretty much ignored it all. Went about in a calm way burning his spiders, tearing wings off flies.

The view from where he stood at the grimy rear window on this tenement landing between the third and fourth floors gave one about as much hope and peace of mind as the hell going on up on the fourth floor: a back parking lot with cracks in the pavement, pot holes and loose cement chunks and gravel that had, over time, become the unofficial dumping site for neighborhood wrecks. Autos of all makes and sizes, pickup trucks, vans, gutted. Some without doors and windshields or wheels, had been abandoned to rust on wood or cinder blocks, bricks, piled rocks.

Knee-high weeds grew from fissures in the pavement. There were scattered stacks and piles of threadbare tires and strips of black rubber throughout; rusted out mufflers, gas tanks, radiators and grills; engines that had long ago been stripped of anything useful.

Down, toward the right-hand part of the parking lot-cum-junkyard, where the dumpster was located and over-flowing to capacity with refuse, dead foliage, and an assortment of fractured and discarded bargain-basement, low-rent coffee tables and nightstands, sofas and chairs, toasters, crock pots, washers and dryers, refrigerators and other appliances, large and small, with additional mounds of plastic trash bags bloated and splitting at the seams, that surrounded it at the base, were a couple of stray dogs engaged in the act, something the boy had been exposed to enough times in the past, so that in and of itself held no real interest; only these two were caught up/entangled in such a way that he had never witnessed until now. Stuck, they were, ass-to-ass, literally; on all fours, heads at opposite ends. Evidently attempting to separate, to untangle, and not able to do so.

One would pull one way for a while, dragging the other with him, then the other mutt would pull, or try to, in his direction, forcing the other dog to back up, neither getting anywhere.

Mexican standoff? He couldn't say. All he knew was it was the Latino part of town. East LA. What was going on?

It was only moments earlier that they had been in front of the building. Fucking, to be sure, but doing it the way they were supposed to: the male, forepaws atop the other's hind end, while he pumped away from behind. The boy's mother, with whom the boy had walked up, having been thoroughly disgusted by the sight, had flung one of her pumps at them. The dogs hadn't bothered to separate—maybe even then had not been able to—instead had hopped the short distance to the left of the tenement to where the driveway and entrance to the lot in back was. And here they were, still at it, only coupled in this baffling manner.

He wondered what was going on, if only in a casual way. Because the mongrels, the junkyard, and the heaps hardly mattered beyond what went on in them at night, as well as during the day: local prostitutes, some who lived in the building, sneaking about with their johns, junkies in a crazy frenzy to slam a needle somewhere, bums seeking out vehicles with missing seats to take a dump in.

He'd taken more than one girl to one of the forgotten sedans himself, gotten them to pull their panties down and show him what they had.

None of that rated this mid-morning. No. What mattered and preoccupied his thoughts were the spiders and fat flies he enjoyed burning to a crisp on his side of the window, the flies who threw themselves mindlessly against the pane, and the spiders lying in wait in various corners of the window frame and the traps they had spun for the purpose of snagging a meal.

The boy stood at the window, book of matches in hand, doing the thing that sent the familiar sensation through him: setting things on fire, living or not; fire did it for him. Even though it was beyond his comprehension how or why the mere sight of fire and destroying things in this fashion had the effect that it did on him, it did not stop him from yearning for more of the same.

Drawing his attention above his head, in a web in the upper right corner of the frame, a newly trapped fly struggled to untangle itself to no avail. Spiders knew what they were doing. The web was sinewy, tough, and this spider's latest victim was not going anywhere.

As expected, the spider emerged soon enough from within its lair. Moved toward the prey. With bated breath, the kid waited until the predator was practically upon the doomed insect before striking the match, reaching up, and roasting them both.

There were other flies he pounced on, clutched in his fist, and dealt with. Large, glistening green flies, who made the loud buzzing, grating noise that added to the thrill, he caught and relieved them of their wings. They were incredibly easy to grab: dumb flies who kept throwing themselves against the grime-streaked glass as if they expected to be able to drill through somehow and escape out there to join up with thousands of their ilk at the dumpster below and anywhere else throughout the lot.

The boy snatched them up, yanked the wings off, and watched with something like inner satisfaction as they kicked out with their spindly legs on their backs, on the sill, kicking out frantically; that enhanced the experience for him. There was no denying it, no explaining it: the combo, fire and subsequent death, not only heightened the senses all around, but clearly left him in a state of arousal, just as there was no denying he felt responsible for what was taking place up there on the fourth floor.

Coco Garcia, the gap-toothed, obese Mexican woman who lived across the way from them in the other apartment and everyone knew to be a prostitute, who had, in fact, turned his mother on to some of her johns, poked her head out through her partially opened door.

"They're at it again, huh, kid? I wouldn't take that off no man. I hope she beats the shit out of his ass this time."

The boy said nothing. Looked up at her, then turned away to mind his spiders and flies. He was down to his remaining match and that bothered him. The big woman shook her head at the ongoing racket. She withdrew back into her place and closed her door.

"Lemme get this straight, bitch: You stayed out all night and a good part of the morning, and all you got to show for it is a handful of change? Why, you ain't even good at whorin'! To call you a whore would be an insult to all the hard-working whores out there! Hear what I'm saying, bitch? You ain't even good at whorin'! You don't rate!"

"It's the boy's birthday, Joe. I wanted to do something for the boy just this once."

"You ain't even got enough coins left here for a bottle of rotgut—"

"He needed shoes, Joe. It's his birthday."

"How many times I gotta hear about the bastard's birthday, goddamn you! I ain't got enough here for a taste, and you got nerve to spend on shoes and birthday cakes and ice cream!"

"Can't you do without this one time? We'll get some money later—"

"Why should I have to do without, bitch? Why should I have to suffer? Didn't I tell you to abort the bastard? Didn't I?"

"There was no money for it, asshole! You drank everything I brought in—like you're doing now!"

"You're blaming me? It's my fault?"

There was a loud slap. The woman screamed. There was tumbling. Someone being thrown against a wall. More screaming and yelling. Mad dogs barked inside the apartment.

Eight-year-old Cecil Omar Biggs stood at the landing between the floors, struck the last match and burned a plump spider with it. Through with that, he was back on the green flies: easy to catch, while they kept at the filthy windowpane, buzzing away. He'd sever their wings and lower them on the window sill on their backs. Liked to watch them kick wildly this way.

He had an unusually large one now. Was desperate to burn it. Went through his pockets in search of matches. Dug up a book, but no matches left in it. Kept searching, found another. A single match left. Struck it. Lowered the flame toward the frantic fly: the fat fucker. He wanted to kill them all. Nothing gave him more pleasure than killing these fuckers. And then he got him but good. The last match. That was it. Gone. All of them. What would he do? Keep catching them and tear their wings off. He'd have to find some more matches somewhere soon. While happening to look up toward the top of the windowpane at a couple of flies banging their heads against the glass, his eyes wandered up toward the ceiling, up there in both corners, large cobwebs, too, but he couldn't reach those. He wished that he could. There were also plenty of dead moths along the window sill that he felt like frying . . . but he needed matches for that.

The landing was littered: beer cans and soda bottles, cigarette butts and empty cartons, bologna packaging and candy bar wrappers, used condoms and Tampons. He shoved his worn sneaker around in there, in search of a possible match, a lighter . . . and found nothing. He cursed. Needed fire. The yelling and fighting in their apartment kept on: more things being broken; his father's dogs barked. Then he heard John Joseph release a deep howl. The apartment door opened like a cannon shot, and his mother, heavily made-up as usual, both eyes swollen, mouth bleeding, with all that wild dark hair flying and not a stitch of clothing on her, scrambled down the flight of stairs toward him.

There was panic and terror in her peepers; even, incredibly enough, to some degree, a kind of glee. He noticed, too, a couple of her front teeth were missing this time.

She descended the stairs in her clumsy, harried way, with John Joseph, drunk and slobbering, nose and jaw bloody, in his soiled OD green army boxers and worn, mis-matched white socks, staggering in the doorway, the birthday cake haphazardly balanced on the palm of his left hand, while he held onto the doorjamb with the other to steady his aim. He cursed and hurled the cake at her, the birthday cake that she'd only bought moments earlier. J.J. sent the cake flying through the air as she neared the landing where the boy stood. The youngster turned his back in time. The cake grazed the top of her head, and a good deal of it deflected and spattered the back of the boy's neck.

"Half a whore!"

"Up yours, faggot!"

The boy's mother continued on down the next flight to make her way toward the lobby below.

"I'll kill you, bitch! Kill the both of you!"

John Joseph ducked back inside, to reappear seconds later with the box the boy's new footwear was in and pitched the shoes, one at a time, at the eight-year-old.

One shoe bounced off the top of the boy's head and went sailing through the windowpane, causing him to pivot enough for the second shoe to nail him between the eyes. The blow sent the kid spinning into the corner, his face buried in his hands. He wasn't crying, merely doing his best to deal with the throbbing pain.

John Joseph Biggs staggered back into the apartment, slammed the door shut, and could still be heard cursing and carrying on at the top of his lungs.

"That's right: kill you both, so help me! Cake and ice cream, when I ain't even got enough to wet my beak! Good-for-nothing, two-bit half-a-whore! Cake and ice cream! No ass-wipe in the crapper, but there she is throwing good money away on nothin'! Out of dog food, out of ass-wipe, nothin' left to drink—and the bitch throws money away with both hands! What I get for marryin' a madwoman! My own goddamn fault, right there. Could've married up—no, not me; I had to marry down! Insane heifer! Probably got Mad Cow. Wouldn't be surprised."

The boy was squatting in the corner of the landing and wiping his bloody nose with the back of his sleeve. There was no stifling the tears by now.

He heard the door to their apartment open again. Looked up to see Juicer Joe leaning against the door jamb and pointing a shaky finger at him.

"What was you doin'? Playin' with matches, boy? How many times I gotta tell you not to play with fire? Wasn't enough you burned our home down—forced us to have to move to a place like this what we can't even afford."

"I wasn't playing with matches."

"Like hell you wasn't. What you sittin' there for like an asshole? Get that twat in here before she goes out and kills herself!" his father yelled at him, barely able to hold onto the jamb, vomit and blood dribbling down his chin. He had one of his barking large mutts with him on a leather belt, the belt buckle end of which he had a difficult time holding on to.

"You heard what I said, Pissy? Go get your mother! What are you waiting for?"

"What can *I* do? She never listens to me. . . ."

The father swiped at his chin with his hand, staggered back inside, to reappear a short while later with a beer bottle. Noticed that a good swallow of brew remained. He drained it, and the bottle was hurled at the cowering boy, caught him across the lower back and knocked him off his feet.

The kid was doubled up on the floor, wincing in pain.

"*You heard what I said, Pissy?* Quit your fakin' and bring that tramp in here before she throws herself under a bus. Wouldn't break my heart any if she did. Trouble is ain't got no insurance on the bitch. Can't never scrape enough together to take out a policy on the confused heifer! Understand what I'm sayin', boy?"

Cecil looked up. Could not move from the pain and remained lying on the littered floor of the landing.

The door directly across the way from their unit opened, and the same tired, wasted street whore who lived there stuck her head out.

"The fuck you want, skank?"

The woman's eyes were about half open, not that it mattered, because the appallingly bad bleach job that was her hair hung over them. She had on a black bra that was several sizes smaller than it should have been and revealed a far greater amount of the flab that made up the enormous bosom than was flattering. The large, moth-eaten black underpants she wore managed to detract even further from the overall bloated and disagreeable appearance. This was a big woman who easily weighed in excess of two hundred pounds.

"Can you spare a drink, J.J?"

"Get your *nasty, hog bitch ass* back in that *smelly sty* you crawled out of. This is family business."

"*Besame culo, pendejo.*" She flipped him the middle finger.

"Who you calling '*pendejo*,' you tub of shit?"

John Joseph yelled at the dog to go after her. The woman withdrew quickly enough back into her place, slamming the door shut in time.

J.J.'s attention was back on the boy. Yanked on the makeshift leash, pulling the dog back, who would not stop barking and tugging on the belt. This was one manic animal. Out for blood. Anyone's blood.

"Get up, you little turd! I'll turn this beast on you, so help me!"

The canine tugged too hard, causing the drunk to trip on his feet and stagger against the door jamb, driving his face into it, exacerbating the bleeding nose. He cursed. Wiped the blood with the back of his hand. The man gave the dog a few whacks on the head with the buckle end of the belt, then pointed at the youngster.

"Get him, Mojo! Get the little snivel snot down there! Get him!"

The dog charged, pulling the drunk to the stairs. Caused him to miss a step, and down he went, falling on his backside and tumbling down the rest of the way to the landing, cursing both: child and dog.

The boy managed to scramble out of the way in time, crying for help, pleading.

"Daddy, don't! Please, Daddy! Please, Daddy, no! I'll get her! Daddy! Daddy!" Clearly wetting his pants by now.

John Joseph rose to his knees, hissing, in a rage. "Who you callin' 'Daddy,' Pissy? If I told you once I musta told you a hunnerd times: I ain't your Daddy, boy! Just 'cause I married that whore mama of yourn that don't make me your Daddy! I ain't nobody's Daddy!"

He probed for something to pick up out of the pile of litter to throw at the kid. Settled for a nondescript bottle. Flung it. Found an empty whiskey fifth. Threw that down the flight of stairs at the fleeing boy. Missed. The bottle hit the wall. John Joseph could be heard shouting over the breaking glass.

"Don't you *never, never, ever* call me 'Daddy,' boy! I didn't ask to be your Daddy! Only married the nasty heifer on account I musta been outta my mind at the time!"

He felt like chasing after the kid. Was in no condition. Only the dog didn't get that. Kept tugging, and forced the man down to his knees once more.

John Joseph rose, kicked the animal, then began whacking away at it with the belt buckle, drawing blood. Yanked hard on the makeshift leash, and made it back up the stairs to the apartment door. Went in. Slammed it shut.

ZOOK

By KIRK ALEX

Blurb & Novel Excerpt

**Some very strange things are taking place
at the New Pueblo Funeral Home . . .**

War vet, Ray Zook, a PTSD afflicted former grunt, is about to regret that he ever set foot in Tucson, Arizona.

All he wants is to gain the courage to face his inner-demons and somehow explain to the widow of his best friend what *really* happened to him during their stint in the military. But when Zook is mugged and takes a temporary job working the night-shift at a crematory run by a couple of unsavory employees, those plans get derailed.

After witnessing a series of disturbing incidents—like the shady "after hours" business taking place—that hurl him into an immoral world of grave robbing, coffin swapping, and even disappearing bodies, Zook finds himself caught in the middle of a twisted power-struggle to control ownership of the funeral home.

If Zook hopes to escape this utter mess with his sanity intact, he must rise above his fears and confront the dark deeds before he ends up back in the looney bin . . . for good this time.

Chapter 1

I had just gotten off the bus and the two of them followed me: the dim-witted young chick with the dishwater hair and the beastly two-hundred-pound butch dyke with her: all tats and rings and studs and chains. Lots of black leather. Blue/black crew cut. Demanding money.

"For what?"

"BJ."

The other one was quiet. Just wasn't there mentally. Didn't seem like it mattered to her, either. It was the bitch built like a dozer who was after my cash. I dared her to take it, which hadn't been a wise move at all. She cold-cocked me. By the time she was done I was on the ground, nearly out. She'd flipped me over on my belly and sat on my back. I could hardly breathe, let alone do much of anything else at this point. She'd taken my wallet, extracted the bills, tossed it back at me. Spit in my direction, and they walked off. With close to eighty dollars of my jack. My roll. A good chunk of it. If it hadn't been for the paper money I'd kept stashed inside my sock I'd have been up the creek. I was, but at least with what remained I'd be able to rent a room, buy something to eat, a newspaper, and look for work.

I had been sound asleep, as comfortable as one can possibly be on a Greyhound bus. Been pulling on a bottle of hooch all the way from

Phoenix. The idea was to stay on in Tucson long enough to beef up the roll and continue on to Ft. Worth. The ex had family there and I hoped that's where she'd ended up. I didn't have a need to connect with her. It came down to my kid. In her early teens by now. Hadn't seen her in years. I'd been to LaFayette, Indiana; Bowling Green, Kentucky; Lawrence, Kansas, and dozens of other towns, large and small. I stayed on the move; perpetual motion seemed to keep the demons at bay—at least I had myself convinced of it. I had war-related nightmares I couldn't shake, and some other things I was trying to live down. Staying on the move seemed to be the answer. Only how in hell do you get away from yourself? I'd been given the boot by more apartment managers and motel desk clerks for kicking the floor and walls in my sleep than I cared to remember.

It was usually some indiscriminate setting, me unarmed, being chased by the enemy in some far-off land. Commies? Mid-East zealots? Your run-of-the-mill America haters? Who knew? Or maybe I was in denial. Unwilling to face my demons. It took a lot to deal with that shit.

That was where they got on, though: Phoenix. The young one: couldn't tell how old, didn't look half bad in tight jeans, pink blouse, although the heavy one with the butch cut made me want to retch. This was one unappealing broad. And wouldn't you know it, she was the one who dropped her sweaty and mean ass in the seat next to mine. She wanted a hit off my hooch. I told her to piss off. Took the occasional nip from the bottle, pulled the blanket up to about my neck. I had no idea how long I'd be staying in Tucson. Didn't know a soul in town, not really. It was just a place to drive through, or maybe spend a week in, look around. Been in the "Old Pueblo" before. Worked as a busser at some sports bar some years back, did a bit of panhandling.

What nudged me awake was the two of them switching seats. Now the young one was sitting next to me. Before the fat one gave up her seat, she whispered in my ear: "My cousin gives great head."

"How much?"

"Forty bucks."

I told her to get lost.

They switched seats, and before I knew it, "cousin" had her hand under my blanket. Inched it slowly toward my crotch and was rubbing it, just running her fingers gently over it, and I'll be damned if my groin didn't begin to stir. All that vino, and there I was: getting wood. She proceeded to unzip my fly. I let her; pretended I was asleep, and let her do what she wanted. I figured if I acted like I was dozing, they wouldn't be able to claim I owed them money later, her and the beast she was with.

She had it out, stroking, slowly, taking her time. Then she ducked her head under the blanket. I let her. Of course, I let her. It had been a while. No love, no sex. Traveling the country on buses, when the money was there, hitching when it wasn't.

She had her tongue on it, licking; then she had the shaft inside, all of it. I didn't have a tremendous whole lot, but it was all right; there were some poor bastards who envied what I did have. You lived with the hand the Dealer laid on you—and this time the Dealer had shown me some kindness, I thought. That head of hers bobbed up and down, not fast, gently, gradually, taking her time. And the fact it was night provided adequate cover. Passengers were zoned out, with the exception of some punk in his teens, across the aisle, watching out of the corner of his eye. Let him. Probably wished he was me, the big shot, getting his nuts off on a Greyhound bus to nowhere.

The licking went on. She played with the head, flicking it thoroughly. This chick had been around, knew her business when it came to licking balls and sucking cock. It had been such a long time, too. Probably did this to get by: sucked off strangers for whatever they could pick up. Who knew? Did it matter? Only I'd had too much wine. Couldn't make it. It was no good. Wine and sex didn't mix, not for me.

She lifted her head. I pulled out my wallet. Extracted a tenner for her effort. She did what she could. Not her fault. Before the young hooker had had a chance to even take a good look at it, the beast, her freakish "relation," stuck her hand in and snapped up the sawbuck. She sniffed it. Looked it over. She was not pleased. Tough, I thought. That was a ten dollar try.

"My name is not Bill Gates and I don't own *Microsoft*. Besides, I never got off."

"You're lying." She yanked her "cousin" out of the seat, and lowered that wide posterior next to me.

"We agreed on forty."

"Like hell we did."

"That was a forty dollar BJ. You never had anything that good in your life."

"How would you know? Maybe I had better." For a fact. Only my ex-wives wanted nothing to do with me, especially the last one. I had no idea where she was. Ft. Worth was nothing more than a guess, a vague one, like all the other towns I'd been to. She'd taken the kid and disappeared off the face of the earth. Could explain the roaming. If I admitted it to myself. I didn't need the exes back, only ached to see the kid. A girl. Must have been six years ago I saw her last. I didn't blame the wife for leaving me. Couldn't take the screaming in the middle of the night, the kicking at the floor with my feet, the times I was stationed out of the country, or stuck in some bug bin here in the states. I drank to fight the demons. Only made everything worse. They had me on *Prozak*, then *Paxil*, at the VA. While I was in the whack ward the wife dropped the bomb: wanted out. I couldn't stop her, didn't try. She never mentioned custody, only because she figured she was entitled. She'd given birth to the child and that was that. Frankly, I was in no shape to take care of a kid, couldn't even take care of myself. I let it go; let them both go. The ex had a man, in fact, had been shagging a neighbor while I was stationed overseas. The way it usually went. I'd had it done to me once before. Kid could be his, biologically. Probably. Don't matter. I treated her like she was my own. You get emotionally attached. Kids are all right. Always wanted a family. Always did. Things kept going wrong somehow. Something would always happen to turn things upside down. This was divorce number three. You know what they say: three strikes and you're out. Three marriages, three divorces. I was defective, a loser. Something was seriously the matter with me. It was the war; it was other things.

"I doubt it." She looked at me. "Not with that nose and those teeth." My nose was bent, both ways, in bar brawls that I usually started and lost, so were my teeth—born with them that way—the ones still there: black, yellow. Of the uppers in front, I had but one left. In the middle.

I pulled the blanket up, and pretended to go to sleep. Only she wouldn't let me.

"Thirty bucks. You can't deny that was worth thirty bucks."

"You got what it was worth. And that's the end of it. I never got rocks. You bitches came on to me. Before I knew what was going on, your nympho girlfriend was molesting my privates."

"You owe us money."

"Fuck off, or I go to the driver."

"He's our friend. That wouldn't get you anywhere."

"What does *he* pay for it?"

"That's a different case. He gets a discount—and has nothing to do with you."

"I feel drained for some strange reason and crave rest." And this time I shut my eyes and kept them shut. I could feel them switch seats again. As she got up, I turned my head, and caught her cousin going down on some geezer way in the back. I guessed the freak was on her feet in order to collect payment, and before I knew it, the young bitch was back sitting beside me. It wasn't long before she had her hand under my blanket again. This time I slapped it away, and she left me alone.

We got off the bus. I had my old backpack; walking down in search of a cheap motel along Drachman. Then I turned down an alley. Big mistake. They'd had friends waiting for them. Indians. Looked like. I was jumped, knocked down. She stood on one side, while one of those drunk Indian friends of hers stood on the other, and they took turns delivering a couple of very effective, if unsteady, kicks to my kidneys. The beast had emptied my wallet, rummaged through the backpack, spat in disgust and left me lying there in the puke and blood.

Welcome to Tucson, Arizona. To be fair, this was no slam against the Old Pueblo, and besides, the bitches had hopped on in Phoenix.

I was up, wiped vomit from my chin. Dug my hand inside my left sock. At least I still had that. Jammed the spare socks and underwear, photo album, toiletries, back in the pack. Checked into a motel, washed my face, showered, then plopped down on the floor and slept the rest of the night and most of the next day when I had to go out and find a bar, or *Circle K*, to buy a can of *Spam* and a 6- Pack of *Red Dog*, a newspaper. At this rate, my money wouldn't last long and I'd be stuck here indefinitely. Taking a look at the job ads was in order.

* * *

nonentity

—A Rant for Those Who Can't—
Presented as a Novel

KIRK ALEX

Blurb & Novel Excerpt

Chance "Cash" Register is a cranky, reclusive, unemployed author who's down on his luck. And with a dwindling bank account, Cash has limited ways to support himself. Stuck with no other choice but to look for work, Cash hops onto his trusty bike and pedals around Tucson in the summer heat searching for a dreaded 9 to 5 job, but not having much luck.

After being repeatedly rejected by those unrelatable, non-creative types, Cash encounters a series of unusual characters, horrible job offers, and the downright sickening prospect of being homeless. Until he lands employment at a local bakery and the experience changes his miserable existence.

This intense, rage-on-the-page novel chronicles three-months in the life of a struggling writer . . .

FOREWORD

You know how it is: you have a job you don't mind at all, only the psychotic assholes are impossible to deal with. And there you are, find yourself hating to go in in the morning. Dreading it. The 9 to 5 gig felt like being stuck in a mental ward eight hours a day, five days a week. WTF?

Like I said: it wasn't the job itself. Packing & shipping smut. Smut was okay by me. It was perfect, actually. Here in Tucson, of all places. Vids were of chicks with big tits, and some even had the behind, you know? Big butts, luscious hangers. And now and then a porn actress would fly in from somewhere from time to time: LA, Florida, even Europe to meet the owner and/or shoot a vid. You better believe it. But the demented, loud mouthed co-workers—some female, some male—made it a living hell for me. The owner, the boss, was okay. Jersey dude, Jewish; was not bad at all, as were some of the others, but the nutcakes were loose cannons, mentally off—and I knew if I didn't get out, I'd end up in a real loony bin; either that or jail. It was that agonizing; draining. Psychologically & emotionally.

And I tolerated it for something like 27 months. Hung in there, just barely. Hung in. Until it felt like my skull was about to explode. I won't go into explaining and/or describing the loose screw mooks here, only to say it was bad and I had to free myself.

And did. Had a few bucks, but when there is no money coming, your savings, you find out, dissipate way too fast—and there you are: dangling. Sweating it out: Can I make rent? Buy groceries? Pay the light bill, and phone? What about a car? I had no car at the time; didn't want one. Got around on a bicycle; well, because all I made went toward this publishing thing. And back then, at the time of writing and self-pubbing *"Taxi Zone,"* the internet (as far as vendors like Amazon, Kobo, B & N were concerned, where you could promote and sell your books) was in its infancy. Sure, running a print ad here and there in some publication was an option, but going that way cost an arm and a leg. So it was out of the question for a small fry like myself.

Well, I published the aforementioned story collection, paperback version, using plastic—that left me in the hole for thousands. You soon realize going the way of some established publishing entity was out of the question. Period. Was this going to stop me from pursuing a dream I'd been aching to make happen since my early teens? This love of books and writing saved my suicidal ass more times than I care to recall over the years.

Suicidal? Why suicidal? Blame it on an effed up upbringing. Beatings. Brutal. Relentless. Went on for years, up until I was 13 & 1/2. The old man had a short fuse & a violent streak. The old lady? Mentally abusive. Later on, it turned out the reason behind (her meanness) was menopause. Oh, she's cool now, kind and even-tempered. And the old tyrant? Six feet under. But yes, he was one angry and violent fuck. But I digress. That's for another book. Merely pointing out what (primarily) drove me in the direction of reading and writing. It was escape. Survival. It was the late, great Charles Bukowski who said: *The first thing writing must do is save your own ass.* And that it did & continues to do so.

I mean this was not the sole reason am attached to books, but one of the main ones. Being creative was a major outlet, beam of light at the end of the tunnel, so on and so forth. Had to have it—or go insane.

Some turn to drugs, booze, religion, you name it. My way was the creative angle. Could've been worse, I always thought. Could've easily ended up a criminal: robbing banks & causing other forms of mayhem. Right? Right. Another reason why I was grateful to books: How else could I have discovered Elie Wiesel and what the nazi bastards did to the Jews & others, or the great works of literature by the likes of Ernest Hemingway, Knut Hamsun, Nelson Algren, Sylvia Plath, Derek Raymond, Henry Miller, Eugene O'Neil, August Strindberg, Ferdinand Celine, John & Dan Fante, Mark SaFranko, et al. How else?

Anyway, where was I? Having left the job to hold on to my sanity, I had zippo cash coming in—and I desperately wanted to hold on to the roof over my head in order to be able to continue writing. Writing was everything, and to pursue it, not for fame or bucks necessarily, but—as stated—to stay alive, I needed to find some kind of gainful employment.

And I hit a brick wall. Had no idea it would be so damn tough. That's an understatement. *Tough?* It was like attempting to scale Mt. Everest without proper gear; no, no—*without any gear.*

What the fuck was the problem? I kept asking throughout the ordeal that is covered in the book. What was it? I didn't get high, was not a heavy juicer; was not a prima donna, was reliable; was not afraid of manual labor—or any kind of labor. Yes, I wrote whenever I could find the time, but I'd always supported myself doing whatever was at-hand. White collar? I had nothing against it, but writing was, I always felt, *white collar* enough. I liked blue collar, or in-between-collar; no problem.

Would I have been happy to be able to support myself scribbling?

Writing my erotica-laced short stories and genre-hopping novels? Of course. Hell yes. But it wasn't happening. And so, a long time ago, I had resigned myself to the realities of life: day job. Paying gig.

Only once I walked away from the warehouse, I soon found out no one would *not only not hire me, but would not so much as give me the time of day.* Nada. Nothing.

And this is where the rage (on the page) comes in; why I call it a rant. Because that's what it was and is: I'm ranting (in the book.) Against what? Not Tucson necessarily, because I am truly fond of the Old Pueblo, as well as the entire state of Arizona—& Southwest in general; no, just angry and raging against the effing injustice of my situation—after years upon years of paying dues.

Started working at a young age & putting money into the system by the time you were 16? So fucking what? Sent to Southeast Asia at 19? Endured a year in the jungles? So fucking what, pal? What's so special about that?

Then all the dead-end gigs and heavy dues. Driving a hack in Chi-town and rat-race hell hole called LA; having endured all types of shit jobs over the decades and having major bucks yanked from my paycheck, the goddamn DES (Department of Employment Security) here would not give me unemployment long enough to land a gig. Why?

This was the reason behind the pissed attitude and frustration, the ranting; although anyone will tell you walking around with a chip on your shoulder is not a good way to go through life. And yes, we all know it, but sometimes life knocks you down once too often and rage is all that's left.

And no, a perpetual state of anger as a way of dealing with what's being tossed at you is not a good way at all. I'd say being patient, easygoing and even-tempered, very often, is best. It really is. Am not saying this to sound positive and/or wise, but stating it as a fact: a good attitude is healthier for *you*—as well as for *those around you.*

I was certainly aware of this fact while it was happening; and yet, *and yet,* there was no denying, no around it: I was a desperate, unemployed *nonentity* dangling by a thread. And that's why the book is so full of: *What the eff is going on here?*

Am just saying: yes, I knew/was aware that my state of mind worked against me. And, fortunately, I did snap out of it & chucked the chip once my luck changed. The other thing is, it was later, probably after I not only landed a job, but *two jobs* and worked my butt off working those jobs, that it truly dawned on me why it took so long to get hired: *my resume.* Certain employers are reluctant to hire anyone they sense is a *"creative type."* Meaning: you can't be reliable, because you probably have your head in the clouds: busy day-dreaming, coming in late or not coming in at all; doing drugs and staying wasted.

Guess what? As mentioned: *that's not me.* Only how do you explain it to someone who won't even say why you're not being considered, and why you're being passed over for the next guy?

You can't, and so you don't.

Like I said: I didn't realize it, truly did not get it was right on my resume & that it was destroying my chances. It was on there: I'd studied filmmaking for a couple of years in my youth back in LA; that so goddamn hurt me and kept me cornered, stuck, desperate and cursing at the gods. That, and the fact I had no local references that anyone could verify, etc.

Yes, the two-plus years I'd spent at the warehouse I could not include in my resume from fear that if anyone called over there I'd be demonized for walking out. So that was out. Never mind that I'd spent the first six months here as a factory hand, back in '96; left that gig to take the smut packing job. So, couldn't even mention the factory, usually (& didn't), couldn't mention the warehouse, usually (& didn't), instead had to claim that I was new in town. LA references didn't rate. Local employers wanted *local* numbers they could call up. I got it. Couldn't blame them one bit. Even so, I still had to figure out how to survive.

But it turned out okay, as mentioned. Eventually. Please keep this in mind once you get into the book and come across the f-bombs, grumbling and desperation, because a kindness here and there did come this "creative type's" way finally—and I was ever-so-grateful.

Kirk Alex
June 27, 2016

"We'll let you know ..."

The search for work continues. Just like before, *déjà vu* all over again. Between a rock and a hard place. No, I was not looking forward to being in this precarious position . . . but here I am. . . .

I was instructed by the unemployment insurance people to be home from 8 a.m. to 11 a.m. this morning for my phone interview.

Okay. I waited and waited. Guess what? The phone did not ring until 4 minutes of. The lady at the other end asked why I left my job, what the reason was. I explained: the cigarette smoke, the badgering, verbal abuse, being sneezed on by certain Russian employees, etc., all that; never said a negative word against my former employer, though. Did not need to. The man was all right by me. Wanted her to understand that.

She said she did. Only it might be a problem for me to get benefits since I left and was not fired.

This is how it goes.

"Keep looking for employment," she said, "and then Friday mail the pink form in to us."

I got it. "Am I entitled to unemployment insurance?"

"We'll let you know after we've investigated this further."

What's to investigate? I felt like saying. There were people at work

I genuinely liked, and there were others, the assholes I could not stomach, nor could they stand me. What is there to investigate?

I worked 27 months without missing a day, without ever being late once. What is there to investigate? *You are going to keep me from getting my lousy one hundred and eighty-two dollars a week for a few months? What is there to investigate? How can the state of Arizona be so goddamn cheap and tight-fisted and miserly and rotten and heartless?* I felt like saying this, but did not. Let's wait, let's get turned down first and then I'll let them know.

There will be plenty of time for that.

And clearly there was no denying that I felt the pinch, the tightening of the screw. I am bound to worry some, be concerned some . . . this is the way my life, this difficult life of dues, has always gone. . . . And they say, some do, *never let them see you bleed.* . . .

This is what I heard somewhere once. Never let them see you bleed. This is what your detractors would enjoy more than anything; it would be frosting on the cake for them. Your first gift to them was leaving . . . and now you are going to add frosting on top?

Think of it.

Well, it occurred to me, I wrote and directed a horror flick once. Why not take a video copy along with you for the next job interview? Take the promotional material, the articles in various publications . . . also take a copy of that anthology you published last year . . . it might do some good. You never know.

Did that. Placed it inside my pack and rode the bike in Tucson summer heat south to Broadway and then west for a mile or so, to a production office. I didn't get very far. They weren't hiring. The guy, pleasant enough, there were three of them, said they did not have any full-time positions available. I was willing to take anything, part-time, or even work without pay (initially) in order to become knowledgeable with latest digital-editing computer equipment. . . . The guy wearing glasses, who was in his 50s, said they had nothing.

Like L.A., almost. Only they are more pleasant about turning you down here. The story of my life.

I go back out, climb back on the bicycle. Ride it home. One turn-down per day is plenty to bear.

* * *

About the Author

Kirk Alex's novel *Lustmord: Anatomy of a Serial Butcher* was a finalist in the Kindle Book Review's Best Book Awards of 2014. He is also the author of *Zook, Fifty Shades of Tinsel*, the story collection: *Ziggy Popper at Large,* the *Love, Lust & Murder* series: *Throwback & Backlash*, the Eddie "Doc" Holiday Private Eye Series, and a few other novels & shorts.

IF YOU ENJOYED THIS BOOK . . .

Dear Reader, if you enjoyed this book, won't you please consider posting a review wherever you deem suitable. Thank you kindly.

9 780939 122752